Walking on Water

THE FIFTH JOURNAL OF THE WALK SERIES

RICHARD PAUL EVANS

SIMON & SCHUSTER

NEW YORK LONDON TORONTO SYDNEY NEW DELHI

Simon & Schuster
1230 Avenue of the Americas
New York, NY 10020

First Simon & Schuster hardcover edition May 2014

SIMON & SCHUSTER and colophon are registered trademarks
of Simon & Schuster, Inc.

For information about special discounts for bulk purchases,
please contact Simon & Schuster Special Sales at
1-866-506-1949 or business@simonandschuster.com.

The Simon & Schuster Speakers Bureau can bring authors
to your live event. For more information or to book an event,
contact the Simon & Schuster Speakers Bureau at
1-866-248-3049 or visit our website at www.simonspeakers.com.

Interior design by Aline C. Pace

Manufactured in the United States of America

1 3 5 7 9 10 8 6 4 2

Library of Congress Control Number: 2014933520

ISBN 978-1-4516-2831-9
ISBN 978-1-4516-2835-7 (ebook)

Photograph on page 89 © Archive Holdings, Inc./Archive Photos/Getty
Images. Photograph is for representative illustrative purposes only.

Acknowledgments

As I wind up this journey, my own as well as Alan's, I wish to thank all those who helped me cross this country, especially my very talented daughter Jenna for her companionship, navigation (both literal and literary), research, and overall brilliance in helping me craft Alan's journey.

Thank you to my agent, Laurie, for her immediate enthusiasm for this series.

I wish to thank those at Simon & Schuster who have done so much to push Alan along: Jonathan Karp, Carolyn Reidy, Trish Todd (and Molly), Gypsy da Silva, Richard Rhorer for suggesting the title of this book, and the Simon & Schuster promotional and sales teams. Thank you to David Rosenthal, who was there at the beginning of the journey and believed that this series was precisely what America needed at this time.

I wish to thank Glenn Beck and Kevin Balfe for helping

to spread the word about this series, as well as Hoda and Kathie Lee.

Blessings to my staff: Lisa Johnson (the angel midwife), Diane Glad (thank you especially for all your help in Florida), Heather McVey, Barry Evans, Doug Osmond, and Cammy Shosted. Thank you to my dear friend Karen Roylance for helping me brainstorm and believe in the mission of this series.

A special thanks to my neighbor, Joel Richards, for sharing his stories from Vietnam. (You've become an action figure to me.) Thank you to Karrie Richards, Madison Storrs, Natalie Hanley, Ally ☺, Kelly Glad (again!), and Alexis Snyder for their assistance with medical research, as well as Ronda Jones for advising us on Danish names, Earl Stine for sharing with us his experiences of biking the Keys, and Ted and Alease at the Inn at Folkston for their warm welcome.

To Karen Christoffersen, the widow of the real Alan Christoffersen, I hope this series has helped heal your heart and kept your love close to you.

Thank you to my family, Keri, David, Jenna and Sam, Allyson, Abigail and Chase, McKenna, and Michael. And Philly. You are my hope, comfort, and reason.

Most of all, thank you to my beautiful readers around the world, who have made this walk possible—especially all those who have gone outside themselves to tell their friends, families, and colleagues about the series. (Please don't stop!) Without your sharing, we never would have reached so many people.

In memory of my parents,
who taught me to walk

Gulf of Mexico
Vero
"FAITH IS THE BIRD THAT SINGS WHEN THE DAWN IS STILL DARK."
– Tagore
Christmas Box Angel
Lottie's Eats
Miami
EVERGLADES
FLORIDA KEYS
Key West
N
E
S
W

We shall not cease from exploration
And the end of all our exploring
Will be to arrive at where we started
And know the place for the first time.

—*T. S. Eliot*

PROLOGUE

When I was eight years old, three days after my mother's funeral, my father found me curled up on the floor of my bedroom closet.

"What are you doing in there?" he asked.

I sat up, wiping the tears from my face. "Nothing."

"Are you okay?"

"Yeah."

My father, who was never comfortable with outward displays of emotion, had no idea what to do with a crying boy. "All right, then," he finally said, rubbing his chin. "Let me know if you need something."

"Why did she have to die?"

My father looked at me pensively, then took a deep breath. "I don't know. We all die sometime. It's just the way it is."

"Is she in heaven?"

I could see him struggling between telling me what I wanted to hear and telling me what he believed. Even at my age I knew that he didn't believe in God. Finally he said, "If there's a heaven, you can be sure she's there."

"What if there's not a heaven?"

He was quiet for a moment, then he tapped his index finger against his right temple. "Then she's here. In our minds."

"I don't want her there," I said. "I want to forget her. Then it won't hurt so much."

He shook his head. "That would be worse than hurting." He crouched down next to me. "It's our memories that make us who we are. Without them, we're nothing. If that means we have to hurt sometimes, it's worth it."

"I don't think it's worth it."

"Would you wish that she had never been your mother?"

"No," I said angrily.

"To forget her would be exactly that, wouldn't it?"

I thought about it a moment, then said, "Will I ever see her again?"

"We can hope."

As hard as I tried not to, I broke down crying again. "I miss her so much."

My father put his hand on my shoulder. Then, in one of the few times in my life that I can recall, he pulled me into him and held me. "Me too, Son. Me too."

⌖

Imagine that you are sitting on an airplane, holding a pen a few inches above a blank journal page. Now imagine that whatever you write will be read by hundreds or thousands of people. Just imagine. What will you write? Will you share some hidden piece of yourself with those unseen souls? Will you impart some wisdom to help them on their journeys? Are you arrogant enough to believe that anything you write could possibly matter? I suppose that's where I am right now.

My name is Alan Christoffersen, and this is the last

journal of my walk across America. For those who have been following my journey from the beginning, you know where I am, what I've seen, and who I've met. You know about my broken heart, the love I've lost, and the one I hope to find. For those who have been walking with me, we've been through a lot together. And we're not through. Not by a long stretch.

◇

For those new to my journey, I began my walk in Seattle seven days after my wife, McKale, died from complications after a horse riding accident. While she was still alive and I was caring for her, my advertising agency was stolen by my partner and my home was foreclosed on. With no place to live and nothing to live for, I considered taking my life. Instead I decided to walk as far away as I could—Key West, Florida. I have already walked nearly three thousand miles to the Florida state line.

Though I'm close to my destination, in some ways, I've never been further from completing my journey. Once again, I'm unexpectedly headed back west. My father had a heart attack and is in critical condition at the Huntington Hospital in Pasadena. Right now I'm sitting on this airplane not knowing if he's alive or dead. It's almost too much to process. He didn't want me to go back out on my walk, but I did. I feel guilty about that. Did he know something was going to happen to him? If I had stayed would it have made a difference? There are too many questions with answers I don't want to know.

By the time you read this, I will have already passed through many of the doors I'm facing right now. Only these words will be stuck in time. And you, like I am now, are alone with these words. Use them as you will. Every life can be learned from, as either a flame of hope or a cautionary flare. I don't know yet which one mine is. By the time you read this, I probably will.

CHAPTER

One

Sometimes our arms are so full with the burdens
we carry that it hinders our view of the load
those around us are staggering beneath.

Alan Christoffersen's diary

My flight from Jacksonville, Florida, landed in Atlanta, where I had a brief layover before changing planes. My second flight was more crowded than my first. The woman in the seat next to mine, the middle seat in a row of three, held a child on her lap. The woman was crying. I noticed her swollen eyes and tear-streaked cheeks as I got up to let her and her young child to their seat. I didn't know what was wrong with the woman, but she was clearly in pain.

She was a few years younger than I was, pretty even though her eyes were puffy and her mascara smeared. I guessed the child on her lap was around two. She was especially active, which added to the woman's stress. After we had taken off, I took out my phone, set it to a game, and offered it to the woman for her child.

"Maybe this will help keep her occupied."

"Thank you," she said softly. "I'm sorry I'm such a mess. My husband died yesterday." She paused with emotion. "I don't know how to explain it to my daughter. She keeps asking for her daddy."

"I'm sorry," I said.

The little girl dropped my phone on the floor. The woman was embarrassed but unable to retrieve it with her daughter on her lap.

"No worries, I'll get it," I said. I unfastened my seat belt, got out of my seat, and picked up my phone.

"Would you mind handing me that bag?" the woman asked.

I lifted a red leather bag from the space on the floor between our feet and handed it to her. She brought out a fabric book and gave it to her daughter.

"Are you from LA?" I asked.

"LA County. I was born in Pasadena."

"I lived next door in Arcadia," I said.

She nodded. "I live in Atlanta now, but my parents are still in Pasadena. I'm going to stay with them for a while."

"It's good to be with family at times like this," I said. "Was your husband's death expected?"

"No. He was in a car crash." Saying this brought tears to her eyes again. She was quiet for a moment, fighting back emotion. Then she said, "The thing is, it was just another day." She shook her head. "Then the police showed up on my doorstep . . ." She breathed in, then exhaled slowly. "It was just another day."

"That's how I felt after my wife died."

"You lost your wife?"

I nodded. "Yes."

"Was it sudden?"

"The accident was. She was thrown by a horse and broke her back. She was paralyzed from the waist down. A month later she got an infection. That's what took her."

"Then you know how I feel."

"Maybe something of what you feel."

The woman closed her eyes as if suddenly lost in thought. A moment later she turned back to me. "Did you love her?"

The question surprised me. "With all my heart."

She looked down a moment, then said, "My husband and I were fighting when he left. The last thing I said to him was 'Don't come back.'"

I frowned. "That's rough."

"They say be careful what you ask for."

"I'm sorry."

She took a deep breath. "Me too. We were probably going to get divorced anyway. I just don't like being to blame for his death."

"You can't—"

"I am to blame," she said. "At least partially. If I hadn't shouted at him, he wouldn't have left. If he hadn't left, he wouldn't have been in the accident. I can't tell you how guilty I feel. I don't know what's worse, the guilt or the loss."

"Did you fight a lot?"

"Constantly." She hesitated for a moment, as if trying to decide whether or not to tell me more. Then she said, "He was a lawyer. I caught him with his secretary parked in a Kroger's parking lot about a mile from his office. I was going to get a coffee when I saw his car and I pulled up behind them. I asked him what he was doing. He said, 'Nothing, we were just talking.' I said, 'In a Kroger's parking lot?' He just stared at me, and I could tell he was making up an excuse. Then he said, 'It's nothing. I forgot one of my briefs and I had her meet me here with it.' I said, 'Do I have *stupid* tattooed on my forehead?'

"His little girlfriend looked so guilty I thought she was going to faint. That night I gave him an ultimatum, fire her or divorce me. He fired her. But I'm pretty sure he never stopped seeing her.

"Two days ago we were sitting together at the breakfast table and it suddenly hit me how alone I was. We were just six feet from each other and we might as well have been on different planets. He was reading the news on his iPad. I told him that I was thinking of going to LA to see my sister; he didn't say anything. Then I said,

'I think I'll probably stay a year or two.' Still nothing. Finally I said, 'I'll probably shack up with my old boyfriend in Irvine.' He looked up and said, 'Who's Irwin?'

"I just looked at him, then said, 'I'm making pasta tonight; try not to be late.' Then I got up and walked out. That night he came home six hours late. I had tried to call him to see where he was, but his phone was off. By the time he got home I had already gone to bed. The next morning he kept apologizing; he said he'd had to work late. But I knew he hadn't been at work because he reeked of alcohol and perfume. Chanel No. 5. How unoriginal is that? I said, 'So how was she?' He looked panicked. Then he said, 'Who?' That's when I told him to get out and not come back."

"And he left?"

She nodded. "Three hours later the police showed up on my doorstep."

"I think most women would have done what you did."

"I suppose." She looked into my eyes. "What happens? There was a time I used to cry when he'd leave me at night. Where does it go?"

"It changes," I said.

"Did it change for you?"

"In ways. Relationships are always changing. My wife and I had our storms, but instead of pulling us apart, they drove us closer together."

"How does that happen?"

"I don't know. I just loved her."

She breathed out heavily. "I wish I could hurt that way." The child had fallen asleep on the woman's lap, and she adjusted her head against her mother's breast.

"Will you stay in Atlanta?" I asked.

"No. The only reason I was in Atlanta was for his job. His funeral is going to be held here. Then I'll have to go back and sell the house and get rid of everything." She looked at her child. "I suppose I'm lucky to have her to keep me focused. Do you have any children?"

"No. We kept putting it off. It's my biggest regret."

She looked down at her daughter and kissed the top of her head. She turned back to me. "So what do you do to forget?"

"You don't forget," I said.

"Then what do you do to survive?"

"I think everyone has to find their own way. I walk."

"You take long walks?"

I hid my amusement at the question. "Yes."

"And it helps?"

"So far."

"I'll have to try that," she said. She leaned back and closed her eyes, pulling her daughter into her. It was maybe five minutes later that she was asleep. I wished that I could have slept too. There was just too much on my mind. She didn't wake until the pilot announced our descent into LAX. After we landed she said, "I never got your name."

"It's Alan."

"I'm Camille."

"It's nice meeting you," I said.

"Thank you for being so sweet," she replied. "I'm glad I sat next to you. Maybe it was a God thing."

"Maybe," I said.

"Keep walking," she said.

I turned my cell phone back on as I walked up the Jetway. I was feeling incredibly anxious, simultaneously eager and afraid to ask how my father was. I went into the men's room and washed my face, then walked back out to the terminal corridor and called Nicole. She answered on the first ring.

"Are you in LA?" she asked.

"I just landed. How is he?"

"He's still in the ICU, but he's stable. He's sleeping now."

I breathed out in relief. "Thank goodness."

"How are you getting to the hospital?"

"I'll take a cab."

"I can pick you up."

"Do you know how to get here?"

"I'll ask one of the nurses."

"I'm on Delta. I'll meet you at the curb."

"I'll call when I get there."

It was good to hear Nicole's voice, even though the last time I'd seen her I'd broken her heart. I wondered how long we'd be able to pretend that hadn't happened. Down in baggage claim, a sizable group was crowded around the baggage carousel even though there were just a few pieces of luggage on it, unclaimed stragglers from an earlier flight.

I walked to the carousel and waited, leaning against a long, stainless-steel coupling of luggage carts as I looked over the eclectic gathering of humanity. McKale once told me that airports were "stages of mini-dramas." She was right. All around me stories played out. There was a joyful reunion of an elderly woman and her children and grandchildren. There were lovers, entwined and impatient to be elsewhere. There was a returned soldier dressed in camouflage, his wife's cheeks wet with tears and his two children holding balloons and a hand-drawn welcome home sign. There were the lonely business-men with loosened ties and tired, drawn faces flush from cocktails, impatiently checking their watches and smartphones.

Camille, my acquaintance from the plane, was half-way across the room from me. She was being held by a tall, silver-haired man as tan as George Hamilton. I guessed he was her father. She said something to him and they both turned and looked at me. She waved and I waved back before they both turned away.

I saw a beautiful young Hispanic woman who re-minded me of Falene. I took my phone back out and replayed the voice mail I'd received just before hearing about my father from Nicole.

"Alan, this is Carroll. Sorry it took so long, but I found your friend. Her phone number is area code 212, 555-5374. Good luck."

My *friend*, he called her. Was that what Falene was? She'd been my executive assistant when my life was good. She'd been my comforter after McKale's funeral. She'd been my support throughout my walk. Then, after ex-pressing her love for me and disappearing, she'd become an enigma. *Friend* was too inadequate a word.

I had hired Carroll, a private investigator and friend of my father's, to find her—which he had. At least physi-cally. Emotionally, I had no idea where she was. I won-dered if she still cared about me. The thought of calling her crossed my mind, but I quickly dismissed it. I was in the middle of enough emotional turmoil. Besides, it was already past 2 A.M. in New York.

It was nearly a half hour before my pack appeared near the end of the long parade of baggage. I lifted it over one shoulder and walked out of the terminal to the curb to wait. Five minutes later my cell phone started ringing. It was Nicole. "Did you say Delta?"

"Yes," I said. "I've got my pack."

"I'm just entering the airport now. I'm driving a red Pontiac Grand Prix."

"I'm near the second exit," I said. "I'll watch for you."

A few minutes later I spotted her and waved. She sidled up to the curb, popped the trunk, then got out of the car. It had been three months since I'd last seen her, and she looked different. She'd lost weight even though she had little to none to lose, and her hair was styled differently. She looked different but pretty. She was always pretty.

I laid my pack on the ground and we embraced. "It's good to see you," she said.

"It's good to see you," I replied. "Thank you for being here."

I threw my pack in the trunk and slammed it shut; then Nicole handed me the car keys. We both climbed in and I drove off toward the hospital. Another hospital— the sixth since McKale's accident. I was spending way too much time in hospitals.

Even though it was October I rolled my window down a little. The night air was sweet and cool. I love California; I always have. But I couldn't believe I was back so soon.

CHAPTER

Two

As happy as I am to see Nicole again, we're living in denial, ignoring the fact that the last time we saw each other I broke her heart. I wonder how long our fiction will last. It's like repairing a leak with duct tape and wondering how long it will hold.

Alan Christoffersen's diary

"How was your flight?" Nicole asked.

"Long." I adjusted the rearview mirror. "How did you find out about my father?"

"We were supposed to have our weekly phone call to go over my finances. You know your father—he's never late, and he never misses anything. So when he didn't call I called his cell phone. A client of his answered. He told me that your father had been rushed to the hospital with a heart attack. He said they'd been at lunch when your father started to complain of chest pains.

"The client had had a heart attack before, so he recognized what was going on. He called 911 and they rushed your father by ambulance to the hospital."

"How did you get down here so fast?"

"I took the first flight from Spokane to LAX. He had just gotten out of surgery when I arrived."

"Thank you for coming," I said.

"I care about him," she said softly. "He's been good to me."

As I listened to her, it occurred to me why Nicole was so close to my father. I had initially assumed it was because of her inherent kindness—which was, no doubt, part of the reason. But her closeness to him transcended mere kindness or friendship. It was something much deeper. She had been close to her own father before he committed suicide. I believe that she was looking to fill that hole—first with her landlord, Bill, the man who had unexpectedly left her a sizable inheritance, then with my father. It made sense. No wonder she had caught the first flight here, and no wonder my father loved her so deeply. She was the daughter he'd never had, and she gladly played the part.

I reached over and took her hand. She put her other hand on top of mine.

"What else do you know about his condition?" I asked.

"Not much. They won't give me the full details since I'm not family. I had to tell them I'm his niece just so they'd let me see him. The doctor will talk to you."

"He's there this late?"

"No. But he said he'll be there in the morning."

"But you've seen my father?"

"Yes."

"How does he look?"

"He looks like he's had a heart attack," she said. "When I saw him he was still pretty drugged up. I held his hand for a while."

"I should have been there," I said. I looked over. "I shouldn't have gone back out. He didn't want me to go. Maybe he knew."

"Don't do that. No one knew. He was glad you were going to finish your walk."

"He said that?"

"Yes. He knew how important it was for you. I know he didn't see that at first, but he came around."

I breathed out slowly. "It really is good to see you again. The last time we talked . . ."

She stopped me. "Let's not go there. I'm here for you. That's all you need to know."

I squeezed her hand.

"So how is the walk going?" she asked.

"One step at a time."

"How far did you get?"

"Almost nine hundred miles. I made it to Folkston, Georgia, just a few miles from the Florida state line."

"Meet anyone interesting?"

"Very."

"More interesting than me?"

"I found a woman who had been tied to a tree by a cult leader. I ended up spending part of the night in their compound and helping another woman escape."

"That's got me beat," she said. "You should write a book about your walk. I'd buy it."

"I'd have to say it's fiction."

"Why is that?"

"No one would believe it was true."

CHAPTER

Three

It is an inevitable and frightening moment in our lives—the day we realize our parents might be as flawed as we are.

Alan Christoffersen's diary

We arrived at the hospital a few minutes past midnight. I had been to Pasadena's Huntington Hospital before. Actually twice. The first time was when I was nine and I'd had pneumonia. The second time was a year later when I was playing punchball at school and broke my arm.

It had been a long time since either of those events, and the hospital didn't look the same as I remembered it.

Following Nicole's directions, I parked near the east tower. We went inside and took the elevator to the second floor.

The corridors in the ICU were wide and lined with glass walls separating patients' rooms. We approached the nurses' station. A tired older woman with tousled hair and wearing dark blue scrubs looked up at me with heavy eyes. "May I help you?"

"I'm here to see Robert Christoffersen."

She pushed a few keys on her computer, then looked back up at me. "Are you family?"

"I'm his son. I just got into town."

"Just a minute." The woman looked back at the screen. "He's in B237."

"Thank you."

Nicole and I walked to the room, stopping outside the door. R. CHRISTOFFERSEN was printed on a sheet shielded behind a plastic holder.

last, fraying line to my past, the sole witness of who I was and where I had come from. It may have been only the emotion of the moment, but somehow I could already feel the growing vacuum.

I had sat there for maybe twenty minutes before Nicole quietly opened the door and slipped into the room. She walked over to the side of my father's bed and gently touched his arm, then came and crouched down next to me. She pulled my head into her neck, gently running her fingers along the nape of my neck the way McKale used to do. She felt good. Comforting.

"Has he woken?" she asked.

"No."

"I'm sorry," she said. Her voice was soft and caring. "Are you okay?"

I didn't answer, which I suppose was an answer. After a few minutes she whispered, "You need to get some sleep. It's late. Especially for you."

"I'll just sleep here," I said.

"Why don't you go home and get a good night's rest? He's not going anywhere."

"Home?" I asked.

"Your father's home."

I looked back at my father's sleeping form. Nicole was right. I was so tired that I could have easily fallen asleep in the chair, but it would have been a miserable night and I was exhausted enough already. "All right," I said. "Where are you staying?"

"At the Marriott," she said. "It's close."

"Why don't you just stay at the house?"

"Maybe later," she said ambiguously. She took my hand. "Come on, let's get you home."

"You go in first," Nicole said. "You should have some time alone with him."

I nodded, then pushed the door open and slowly stepped inside. The room was dark, lit indirectly by a fluorescent panel behind the bed and the lights of the monitors. It smelled of antiseptic.

The man in the bed didn't look like my father. His usually perfectly coiffed hair was uncombed and matted to one side, and his chin was covered with stiff gray stubble. He looked old. Too old. It had been only seven weeks since I'd last seen him, but he looked like he'd aged years. He had an IV tube taped to his arm and an oxygen tube running to his nose. His mouth was partially open as he snored.

I just stood there, looking at him. It was hard to believe that this was the same man who had towered over my childhood like a giant—solid and unyielding as a granite fortress. I gently touched his arm, but he didn't wake. After a few minutes I sat down in one of the padded armchairs near the side of the room.

After a while I glanced down at my watch. It was five minutes past twelve, California time, three in the morning eastern time. Exhausted, I slumped back in the chair. I'd come completely across the country to be with him, but I felt like I was still miles away.

A wave of sadness washed over me, and my eyes welled up. I had been worried about leaving my father, but the truth was, he was leaving *me*. Maybe not tonight, maybe not even this year, but things were changing. Time was gaining on us.

The possibility—the eventual inevitability—of h' death would mean more than just losing my father. would be the end of the world I had known, a world or inhabited by my mother and my wife. My father was

I stopped at the foot of the bed and looked at my father, then touched his leg. "I'll see you in the morning, Dad," I said softly.

He groaned lightly, but never opened his eyes.

~

On the way to the parking lot I handed the keys back to Nicole and asked her to drive. Neither of us said much on the way to my father's house. I was just too tired, emotionally and physically.

With the exception of the front porch light, which came on automatically, the house was dark. The first thing I noticed was that there were leaves on the lawn. Of course there were leaves on every lawn on the street, but on my father's lawn they were as out of place as penguins. My father didn't abide unraked leaves. After I turned ten, it was my job to see that our lawn was free of them, a responsibility he taught me to take seriously.

Nicole said, "I forgot his house key."

"No worries," I said. "My father always keeps one outside for emergencies."

"Are you sure?"

"If the key isn't there, it would be the only thing he's changed in the last seventeen years."

"Wave if it's there," she said, reaching over to unlatch the trunk. "Then call me in the morning when you want to go to the hospital."

"If my dad's car's here, I'll just drive myself."

"Let me know," she said.

"Thank you," I said. "Good night."

"Night," she replied.

I retrieved my pack from the trunk, then crunched through the leaves to the house. At the front porch I laid down my pack, then squatted down and reached behind the potted kumquat tree next to the door, my hands groping around its flaking plaster circumference. As I expected, the house key was there—just as it had been when I was sixteen. My father had placed it there when I started dating so I wouldn't have to wake him if I forgot my keys.

I waved to Nicole, and she backed out of the driveway. The car's headlights flashed across the front of the house as she pulled into the street. I unlocked the door and stepped inside.

CHAPTER

Four

The further along we get on our life journey
the more we wonder about those who traveled
before us and paved the road.

Alan Christoffersen's diary

The house was as dark as a cave, which wasn't surprising. If my father had a religion, it was thrift, and to leave a light on was a cardinal sin. But at that moment the dark seemed greater than the lack of light. There seemed to be a lack of *life*, a vacuum of energy. Even after I had turned on the foyer light, standing in the silent and cold entryway filled me with a sense of foreboding. The house felt different than it had just a couple of months earlier when I'd stayed there. Now it felt less like a home and more like a museum. Or a mausoleum.

I laid my pack against the wall, then adjusted the thermostat, which, in spite of the month, was turned all the way down. I waited until I heard the furnace kick in; then I walked to the end of the hallway to my father's bedroom and turned on the light.

Not surprisingly, his room was immaculate. The bed was made with tight military corners, covered in a bedspread that I recognized from my youth. My mother had purchased the spread in the eighties—several years before she died and my father and I moved to California. My father just didn't buy things like bedspreads or linens. He was pragmatic that way. If an object still fulfilled its purpose, there was no reason to replace it. A few years back, when I had suggested that he get a new couch to replace the ancient one he'd had for as long as I could remember, he replied, "What's wrong with this one? It still keeps my butt off the floor."

The austerity of his room highlighted what few pieces of art he possessed. On top of his bed stand was a statue I'd never forget—a twelve-inch resin replica of Rodin's *The Kiss*. The lovers are, of course, nude, and, when I was a boy, the figurine embarrassed me more than I could bear. I remember once sneaking into my father's room with McKale. I had told her about the statue and, to my dismay (actually, horror), she said she wanted to see it. We stood there, next to each other, just staring. Finally McKale said, "It's beautiful."

I was dumbstruck. In the sexual naïveté of youth I had just figured that my dad was a pervert. Now McKale was too? Or maybe something was wrong with me. It was all so confusing. "Really?" I finally said.

"Someday I want to kiss someone like that."

Hearing her say that made me feel funny inside— something I wouldn't understand for a few more years.

On the wall closest to the foot of the bed was a homemade decoupage plaque, an uncharacteristically crafty piece my father had made for my mother when they were poor and first married.

Kate,

Wherever you are, wherever you go, I love you and I always will.

-Bob

Something was different about the plaque. There had once been a seashell mounted on the side, but it was now gone, leaving an exposed patch of faded wood and hard, yellowed resin. I looked around on the floor, wondering if the shell had fallen off, but it wasn't there. This was a detail my father would not have missed. It bothered me that the shell was missing.

Outside of the statue, I suppose the plaque was about the only evidence I had that my father was capable of romance—not that the lack of evidence bothered me. The idea of parents having a romantic relationship has been nauseating children for millennia.

I knew my parents locked their door now and then, and I had some idea that something dodgy might be going on inside, but, again, to a child that doesn't equate to romance. Just weirdness. So the fact that I never saw my father be affectionate with my mom didn't register with me until I was older and had started dating McKale. One night I asked my father why I had never seen him kiss Mom.

"We kissed. It just wasn't any of your business," he said gruffly. "Or anyone else's."

For so many years my father had slept without the warmth of a wife. My heart hurt for him and his years of loneliness. No wonder he had wanted me back.

On his nightstand was something out of place—a white plastic binder. I walked over and picked it up.

CHRISTOFFERSEN FAMILY HISTORY

Compiled by Robert A. Christoffersen

My father had never told me that he was working on a family history. I opened the binder. The title page read:

CHRISTOFFERSEN FAMILY HISTORY
(1882–20—)

I turned the page. There was a drawing of a five-generation family tree.

The next page was an official-looking genealogical form that started with me and went back four generations. In spite of my exhaustion I wanted to read on, but I considered that perhaps my father meant to surprise me with it. Why else wouldn't he have told me about such a major project?

I turned out the light and walked down the hall to the guest room. I pulled off my clothes, leaving them in a pile on the floor near the door, then climbed into bed.

As I lay there in the dark looking up at the ceiling, my mind reeled with questions. How was this all going to play out? How long would it be until my father came home again? Why did I feel like such a stranger in the home I grew up in?

The house didn't feel right without my father. He needed to get better. He needed to come home. Something told me that he wouldn't.

CHAPTER

Five

My father has more women waiting outside
his door than a Nordstrom's before a sale.
I wonder why he's never been caught.

Alan Christoffersen's diary

I woke the next morning with the sun. I hadn't checked my watch before bed, but I had probably gotten less than five hours of rest. I was more eager to see my father than I was to sleep. I took a quick shower and shaved, then dressed in the last of my clean clothes—a pair of jeans and a polo shirt.

I dumped my pack out onto the laundry room floor, threw my socks, underwear, and T-shirts into the washing machine, added the requisite chemicals, and turned it on.

Then I checked the garage. I was glad to find my father's twelve-year-old olive-green Buick Riviera parked inside. I went back to the kitchen and looked for the car keys in the drawer where he always kept them, but they weren't there. Then I remembered that someone else must have driven the car home. I went back out to the garage and found the keys on the driver's seat. I put them in my pocket, then texted Nicole.

Have car. Meet you at hospital.

She texted back almost immediately.

Be there in 45

I looked inside the refrigerator for something to eat. My father kept a lean fridge, and, besides the usual condiments, there was only fruit, milk, an open box of baking soda, and two packages of batteries.

In the pantry there were two boxes of cereal, Cheerios and Wheaties. As a boy I'd begged my father for the sugar cereals—Cap'n Crunch, Trix, the good stuff—but he never gave in. My father was anti-sugar long before the cereal manufacturers began pulling the word from the front of their boxes.

I poured myself a bowl of Wheaties, drowned it in milk, and wolfed it down, wondering what my father found so remarkable about the cereal. It occurred to me that that was probably the point—it was completely *un*-remarkable, as practical a use of grain as imaginable. I put my bowl in the sink, then turned off all the lights in the house. It was time to go see my father.

As I opened the front door I was surprised to find a woman standing on the front porch. She was in her late forties and attractive. She was dressed in a form-fitting, baby-blue running outfit, her blond hair pulled back in a ponytail. She was holding a basket of muffins. I must have looked surprised.

"I'm sorry to startle you," she said. "You must be Alan."

"Yes."

"It's nice to finally meet you. I've heard so much about you. Is your father home?"

"No. He's not here."

She frowned. "I heard that he"—she grimaced—"had some health problems . . . When I saw the lights on, I thought maybe he was back. How is he?"

"He's had a heart attack, but outside of that I don't know. I'm headed to the hospital now."

"I won't keep you," she said, holding out her basket. "I baked some muffins for your father. Please tell him that Susie sends her love and best wishes."

"And muffins," I added, taking the offering. "Thank you."

"Thank you. Bye."

She turned and walked back to the road. I wondered how many women my dad had chasing him. I'd wager dozens. He was handsome, fit, and solid as a savings bond. I locked the door, then drove my father's Buick to the hospital.

CHAPTER

Six

The doctor has informed me that what my father has suffered is sometimes called "the widow maker." In my father's case the term is irrelevant.

Alan Christoffersen's diary

The Huntington Hospital was less than a fifteen-minute drive from my father's house. In spite of its age, the hospital was modern looking and bright—well lit from an abundance of window space. I took the elevator to the second floor and walked up to the nurses' station. The nurse sitting behind the counter glanced at the basket of muffins, then back at me. "May I help you?"

"I'm here to see my father. Robert Christoffersen."

"Robert Christoffersen," she repeated. She looked at her screen while she typed in the name. "Your father's doctor is in this morning. I have a note that you'd like a consultation. Would you like me to page him?"

"Yes. Please."

As I stood there, Nicole walked out of the elevator. Even though her eyes were still heavy, she looked pretty with her hair pulled back. She smiled when she saw me.

"Good morning," I said.

"Good morning," she echoed.

I set the muffins down on the counter and we hugged. "Have you seen your father?" she asked.

"Not yet."

The nurse said, "Excuse me. Dr. Witt is on his way."

"Thank you," I replied. I turned back to Nicole. "I'm going to meet with the doctor first."

She grinned. "Looks like you stayed up to bake muffins."

"Yeah, right. A woman came over this morning bearing gifts."

"I'm not surprised. Your father has women chasing him from all over," Nicole said.

Just then a man wearing a white coat over mint-green scrubs walked up. He was tall and thin with slightly graying temples. He was probably only a few years older than me. "Are you Mr. Christoffersen?"

"Yes."

"I'm Dr. Witt," he said, extending his hand.

"Call me Alan," I said.

He looked at Nicole and smiled. "This is your wife?"

"No," Nicole said. "I'm a friend of the family."

He nodded. "All right, let's find a room to talk."

I retrieved the basket of muffins, and Nicole and I followed the doctor down the hallway until he stopped and opened a door. "This will do."

Nicole touched my arm. "May I listen in?"

"Of course," I said.

"Have a seat," the doctor said, sitting down on an examination stool. His demeanor turned more serious. "I don't know how much you already know, so I'm just going to walk you through the events of the past few days. Your father has suffered a serious heart attack. When he arrived in emergency we ran a catheter up through his femoral artery to his heart, looking for blockages. We found one, so we placed a stent in the artery to open it and allow the blood to flow through. He was then brought up here to the ICU, where we started him on medications to help his heart pump.

"The next morning we ran an echocardiogram. We do this to make sure the entire heart is functioning normally, or, if it isn't, to find where there might be muscle damage." His expression fell a little. "Frankly, what we found wasn't good. What your father had was a very serious type of heart attack—a blockage to the LAD."

"What's that?" I asked.

"LAD stands for left anterior descending artery. This type of blockage is sometimes called the widow maker, because the LAD is responsible for supplying blood to the left ventricle, which is primarily responsible for pumping blood to the rest of the body. If this area of the heart is oxygen deprived for a long time, the heart won't pump effectively, which is what we term heart failure. There's been damage; we're just not sure of the extent."

Nicole looked afraid.

"What do we do now?" I asked.

The doctor breathed out slowly. "Right now, it's a bit of a game of wait and see. As I said, we've got him on medications to help his heart pump. As long as he's being given these medications he'll have to be monitored closely, which means he'll be required to stay in critical care. If his condition improves, we might send him to a step-down unit. But for now, we just need to see how his body responds to his treatment. Fortunately, aside from his heart issues, your father is in good physical condition. Otherwise he probably wouldn't still be with us."

Nicole took my hand. The doctor looked at her, then back at me. "I'm sorry the news isn't better. But your father's a strong man. I wouldn't be surprised to see him recover. I'll keep you informed. Are you in town for a while?"

"Indefinitely," I replied.

"Good. It always helps to have family near. We'll keep our fingers crossed."

"Thank you," I said.

"Yes, thank you," Nicole said.

"You're welcome," he replied. He looked at us for a moment, then said, "I need to check on a patient. You're welcome to stay in here if you like."

"Thank you," Nicole said again. He smiled at her, then stood and walked out of the room, leaving my head spinning a little. Nicole wiped a tear back from her cheek.

"Are you okay?" I asked.

"I'm sorry," she said. "I should be comforting you."

After a moment I stood. "I'm going to go see him now. Do you want to come?"

She stood too, then grabbed a couple of tissues from a box on the counter and wiped her eyes. "You go ahead. You two need some time to catch up." As I started to walk out she said, "Don't forget the muffins."

I grabbed the basket from the counter and walked down the hall to my father's room. I set the muffins on a stand near his bed, then stood at his side, watching him. A monitor beeped with his heart, and I could see its motion on a digital screen. My father's life was that jagged little green line on the monitor.

It was several minutes before his eyes flickered, then opened. For a moment he just looked at me, as if he wasn't sure who I was.

"Hi," I said softly.

He swallowed, then pursed his lips, wetting them with his tongue. "What are you doing here?"

"Nicole called."

"Did you finish your walk?"

"No."

"Why not?"

"Because Nicole called."

"You came all the way back because I was in here?"

"Of course I did."

He closed his eyes again and slowly breathed out. "You should have finished your walk. Let the dead bury the dead."

"You're not dead," I said.

"Not yet," he replied.

I raked my hair back with my fingers. "What does that mean anyway? The dead don't do burials. The dead don't do anything but rot."

"No one knows," he said. "It's in the Bible."

"Since when do you read the Bible?"

"I read a lot of things," he said. "Fiction and nonfiction."

I almost asked him which one he considered the Bible to be, but I held back. "Your neighbor came by. She brought some muffins."

"Diane?"

"No."

"Who?"

With so much on my mind, I had already forgotten her name. "I don't remember. She was blond. Pretty."

"Susie?"

"That's the one," I said. "How many girlfriends do you have?"

"None that I know of. They just come over some- times. Susie's a divorcée. I help her with stuff around the house sometimes and we play tennis every now and then. Tell her thank you if you see her again."

"She's a beautiful woman."

"How far did you get?"

I grinned. "With Susie?"

He didn't smile. "On your *walk*."

"Florida."

"Did you walk through the Okefenokee Swamp?"

"Not through it. Around it."

"On Highway One?"

"Yes. You've been there?"

"No. Almost."

More silence. He reached up and adjusted the oxygen tube that ran to his nose.

"Do you need any help?" I asked.

"No." He put his hand back down. "They've got me strung up like a marionette. Has the doctor talked to you?"

"Yes."

"What did he tell you?"

"He said you're going to be okay."

"You don't need to lie. I know what happened. Damage to the LAD. They call it the widow maker."

"He didn't say you were going to die."

"They never tell you you're going to die."

"They tell people they're going to die all the time," I said. "*If* they're going to die."

He didn't reply.

"I'm not lying," I said. "I'm just more positive than you are."

"I'm positive," he said. "That I'm probably going to die."

"That's not helpful," I said.

"I'm not trying to be helpful. I'm being honest."

"Being negative is no more honest than being positive. You should be more positive. Attitude is everything. You always used to tell me that. How would you have felt if I had talked that way when I was in the hospital?"

"Which time? You spend so much time in hospitals these days I'm thinking of buying you your own gown and having it monogrammed."

I shook my head. "You're cranky."

He was quiet a moment, then said, "You're right, I wouldn't have liked it. Sorry."

"It's okay," I said.

"Where are you staying?" he asked.

"At the house."

"Smart. Did you turn the lights out?"

"Of course." I took a deep breath. "I noticed that you're working on your family history."

"You went into my room?"

"I'm sorry. I just . . ." I stopped. I wasn't sure why I had gone into his room. "What brought this on? The family history . . ."

"I don't know," he said. His voice softened. "There's just something about getting older. You feel yourself drawn back."

"Back where?"

"Back to your roots. When you get older something makes you want to know where you came from. Who knows? Maybe it's a way to compensate for not knowing where you're going." He rubbed his chin. "These days they have all these online genealogy sites. I've met some relatives I didn't even know I had. It's been nice catching up."

"Why didn't you tell me you were doing this?"

"You weren't around."

"I was here for two months. You never once mentioned that you were working on your history."

"I didn't think you'd be interested."

"I'm interested."

I sensed that he was pleased.

"Do you mind if I read what you've written?"

"No. Of course not. Who else would want to?" A moment later he asked, "Is Nicole here?"

"She's in the hall."

"Good," he said. "She's a good girl." He looked at me thoughtfully. "Was it hard seeing her? After your last parting?"

"It was a little awkward. But she's been great."

"She has a heart of gold," he said. He paused a moment, then asked, "How about Falene? Did you find her?"

"Your friend Carroll found her. I haven't talked to her yet."

"Why not?"

"He just called yesterday. There was already too much on my mind."

"You mean with me?"

"Yes."

He took a deep breath. "You don't need to worry about me."

"I do worry . . ." I paused, suddenly filled with emotion. "I'm sorry I left. I should have been there for you."

He looked at me for a moment, then said, "No. You did the right thing. You couldn't have seen this coming. Hell, I didn't see it coming. I've been eating wheat bread and egg whites for the last ten years, I jog two miles every day and never miss my morning calisthenics. I thought I was going to live forever." He shook his head. "No, you did the right thing. You need to finish your walk."

The room fell into silence. After a while he said, "Why don't you tell Nicole to come in?"

"I'll get her," I said.

I walked out into the corridor. Nicole was standing near the door clutching a crumpled Kleenex. She looked up at me as I came out. Her eyes were swollen. "My dad wants to see you."

"I don't know if I should go in," she said. "I can't stop crying."

"It'll be okay," I said. "He wants you there."

She wiped her eyes one more time, then walked to the side of my father's bed and reached over the rail to take his hand. "Good morning," she said.

"It is," he said. "I'm with my two favorite people." He looked into her eyes. "Why are you crying?"

She shook her head. "I don't know. I'm a crier."

"Me too," he said. "It's a curse."

In spite of her tears, Nicole started laughing. Then my father did as well. "Come give me a hug," he said. "Does this rail thing go down?"

Nicole dropped the side railing, and my father extended his arms toward her. She put her head on his chest and he put his arms around her, consoling her. She broke down crying. After a while she leaned back and wiped her eyes. "I'm sorry."

"Don't worry," he said. "Everything will be okay."

"I know," she said. "I know you will."

"So what's on the agenda today?" I asked.

"I have no agenda," he said.

"How about some chess?" I said.

"Chess will do." He looked at Nicole. "Do you want to play?"

"I'll watch," she said.

The hospital had a chess set, and my father and I played just one game before he stopped to take a nap. He won, of course. I had never beaten him at chess. Even when I was young and he was teaching me he showed no mercy.

I stayed with him for the rest of the day, except when I went down to the cafeteria for lunch and Nicole spelled me.

He woke around two and ate lunch. We talked for several more hours, mostly about the last leg of my walk, though several times while we were talking he dozed off, once in the middle of a sentence. A nurse came in to check his vitals, and I asked her if sleeping this much was normal. She assured me that it was.

My father fell asleep around four and didn't wake again until after six. He looked surprised to see us.

"What are you still doing here?" he asked. "Afraid you're going to miss something?"

"We didn't want to leave you alone," Nicole said.

"I've spent most of my life alone," he replied. "Why change things now? Besides, you've seen how often these nurses come banging in here. I couldn't be alone if I wanted to."

"Maybe we don't want to go," Nicole said. "You think it's always about you?"

My father smiled. Nicole knew how to talk to him. While he ate his dinner, I helped him search the television for a channel with boxing. After he had settled in, Nicole and I said good night. Nicole kissed him on the cheek. "I'll be back in the morning."

"Don't come too early," he said. "It's a waste of your time. And you need your rest. You look more tired than I do."

"Don't be so bossy," she said. He smiled at her. She squeezed his hand, then left the room.

My father said to me, "Good night, Son."

"Night, Dad. See you in the morning."

As I started to walk out he said, "Al."

I turned back.

"I'm glad you're here."

"Me too."

Nicole was waiting for me in the hallway. "Want to get some dinner?" I asked.

"I'm glad you asked," she said. "I'm starving."

"Good," I said. "I know a place."

CHAPTER

Seven

Over dinner Nicole asked about Falene, which
spoiled my meal as effectively as if she had
poured the entire shaker of salt on it.

Alan Christoffersen's diary

DiSera's is an authentic little Italian restaurant with a wood-fired pizza oven, red checked tablecloths, paper menus, and centerpieces made from candles melted over empty wine bottles. There were black-and-white, framed photographs of pretty Italian girls on vintage Vespa scooters and a series of pictures of a young Sophia Loren.

The food was cheap and good, and even though my father and I didn't eat out much, we had eaten here more times than I could remember. I had taken McKale here at least a dozen times on dates.

After the waitress had left with our order, Nicole asked, "Are you okay?"

"I'm all right."

"It must be hard seeing your father like that."

I nodded. "When you're young you think of your parents as omnipotent—like Oz the Great and Powerful. Seeing him like this is like seeing the little man behind the curtain."

"I know what you mean. I think every son or daughter eventually experiences that."

"He's been writing his family history."

Nicole nodded. "I know. He told me a few weeks ago."

I thought it peculiar that he'd tell her but not me. "I asked him why he was doing it. He said something was just drawing him to it. Mortality."

Nicole shook her head. "He has plenty of life left in him."

"I hope you're right." I took a drink of ice water. "How long are you going to stay?"

"As long as he needs me."

"That could be a while," I said.

"I know. I have the time."

A few minutes later our waitress brought out our food, and we ate awhile in silence.

Nicole suddenly asked, "Did you find Falene?"

I looked up at her. "Just a few days ago."

"How is she?"

"I don't know. I haven't talked to her yet. I've been too worried about my father."

Nicole didn't say anything, and I couldn't tell what she was thinking. Fortunately, she didn't say anything more about Falene. After dinner I drove Nicole back to her car in the hospital parking lot.

"Thank you for dinner," she said.

"My pleasure."

She looked sad as she lifted her purse. "Where did I put my key?"

"Why don't you just stay at the house?" I said again. "It will get expensive staying at a hotel."

"You sound like your father."

"Is that bad?"

"No," she said. "I'll think about it."

From the way she said it I was pretty sure she had already made up her mind not to. She rooted through her purse until she found her car key. "Found it. I'll see you in the morning."

"Good night," I replied.

She waved as she drove off to her hotel.

I suppose it was no mystery why she didn't want to stay at the house. I couldn't give her what she wanted. I loved her, but I wasn't *in* love with her. I don't know why. She was beautiful, kind, loving, and fun to be with. In spite of Falene, part of me wished I were in love with Nicole. It would certainly have made things easier. Unfortunately, the heart rarely takes requests.

CHAPTER

Eight

The roots of a family tree are oftentimes
more twisted than what we see above ground.

Alan Christoffersen's diary

It was a little after ten when I pulled into the driveway. There was a package on the porch about the size of a shoe box. It was from someone named Pam. As I unlocked the door, I noticed another package lying sideways in the bushes. I practically had to climb over a bush to lift it out. There was a card on top. It was from another woman. Margie. I grinned. Pam was ruthless.

I walked into the kitchen and set both of the women's packages on the counter, then went to the laundry room. I moved my underwear, socks, and T-shirts to the dryer and put in another load to wash. Then I walked to my father's room and retrieved his family history, carrying it back to my own room. I lay on my bed and began to read.

INTRODUCTION

The history of a family begins with a name. Throughout history the name Christoffersen has been recorded in more than seventy different derivations, including Cristofori, Kristofer, and Christof. One might easily conclude that the Christoffersen name is of Christian origins, but that is incorrect. Christoffersen is of pre-Christian origin, derived from the Greek word *kristos*, which literally means "leader." The Roman *Christopherus* is also from Greek with the added *pher*, which means "to follow." So Christoffersen literally means "leader to follow."

While the name did not originate with Christianity, it was adopted by the Crusaders, who gave their children biblical names. Our surname, Christoffersen, is a variation of the Danish Kristoffersen.

I
Jon Kristoffersen/Finn Christoffersen

My great-grandfather, Jon Kristoffersen, was born in rural Denmark in 1882. He was the fourth of seven children and (as far as available records show) the only one in his family to emigrate.

Jon was born into a time of economic turmoil. Throughout the mid-1800s the Danish population had grown dramatically due to what some historians referred to as "the danger of peace, prosperity, and population." Peacetime, combined with the introduction of vaccinations and the abundance of potato crops, drastically decreased mortality rates, creating a population surge that the country's economy could not support. While these advances had many positive effects on the Danish people, they also created economic hardship for families like the Kristoffersens, who supported themselves through farming. Family farms could only be passed on to one child (typically the oldest son), which created a predicament, as most Danish farming families had many children.

Children from families like the Kristoffersens knew there was little hope that they would ever gain the capital needed to buy their own farms, and jobs outside of the family farm became scarce as more and more children of farmers became adults and sought to make their own way in the world. When Jon came of age, he found work as a farmhand for a very low wage and kept his eye open for something better.

Around this time a wave of Danes began immigrating to the United States. Their letters home described a land of opportunity where the government sold large tracts of land and a man could become successful so long as he worked hard. Danish newspapers began publishing the letters, and although many of their claims were exaggerated, they were effective in catching the attention of young men like my great-grandfather, who decided to immigrate to the United States.

At that time most immigrants traveled by steamship, and although the trip would take only ten days, it took Jon more than a year to save up for the journey. He left Denmark through the port of Copenhagen on July 7, 1901. He was nineteen years old, and it was the last time he would ever see his homeland. Two weeks later he landed at Ellis Island. It is unknown whether the spelling change of Kristoffersen to Christoffersen was initiated by my great-grandfather, immigration inspectors, or mistakes in the ship's manifest, but the immigrant logs show that Jon's name was recorded as Jon Christoffersen.

Jon followed the example of many other immigrating Danes and made his way to the Midwest, where he found work in Minnesota as a farmhand for another Danish immigrant, Poul Johansen, who raised cattle and hogs. Jon earned double the amount he had in Denmark. His plan was to work the ten years necessary to earn the money for his own farm, but his plans changed when he fell in love with Johansen's daughter, Lena, who was seventeen when Jon began working for her father. Just a year later they were married. They lived on Johansen's farm, where Lena gave birth to their first child, Finn, in 1903.

Once again, Jon was swayed by promises of a new and better life farther west. He left farming behind for good when he and Lena decided they would travel nearly one thousand miles west to Butte, Montana, to start a new life. They had heard that several major mines had recently struck gold (true) and that all the miners were getting rich (not so true).

In 1908 Butte was a bustling Western town of more than sixty-five thousand inhabitants, where, as Will Rogers wrote, men "still wore ten-gallon hats and red neckerchiefs."

While gold was what drew men to the area, copper was what kept them there. Jon got a job at the Anaconda Copper Mine and worked there for the rest of his life.

Shortly after their arrival in Butte, Lena gave birth to two more children, another boy, Lars, who died from fever at the age of three, and a girl, Hanne, who was stillborn. After the loss of two children, Lena was so heavily grieved that some thought her "touched." The family's surviving child was sensitive to his mother's pain, as observed by his father:

> *Finn is a sensitive and melancholy child. He is much endeared to his mother and seeks to earn her love, which she withholds not out of spite, but because her broken heart has none to give.*
>
> —Diary of Jon Christoffersen

Finn was a hardworking and enterprising young man. At the age of twenty-one, he opened his own grocery store, which prospered. That same year he married Genevieve Crimmons, a young woman from a second-generation Butte Irish family. While he was looked down on by Genevieve's parents, Finn was lauded by his own family for marrying into an established local family. Finn seemed to have realized the American dream. A year after they married, Genevieve gave birth to their first child, a girl whom they named Paula. Genevieve was a demanding woman and wanted more than her husband could provide. She convinced Finn to abandon the business, although Jon counseled against it. Finn and Genevieve extended the family's western migration to the larger city of Seattle, Washington, where her aunt and uncle lived. Here, they thought they could have greater income, and they opened a new store.

I found it interesting that I was not the first Christoffersen to go to Seattle looking for greater opportunity.

Less than a year after Finn's family moved, Jon contracted yellow fever and passed away. He was followed only a week later by his wife, Lena. Finn was unable to return to Butte for his own parents' funerals, as the store was highly demanding—almost as demanding as his wife. In spite of his best efforts, the store did not do well. In the meantime Genevieve gave birth to two more children, both boys: Peter and Thomas.

In October 1929, just four years after their relocation to Seattle, the Great Depression hit. As was the case with thousands of enterprises, Finn's store failed. Creditors demanded payment or took back their wares, sometimes both. Genevieve's complaining became intolerable, and she blamed Finn for their family's suffering. According to Finn's journal, he was kicked out of their marital bed. Genevieve was cruel.

> *Genny was at me again tonight. I long for her affection but*
> *am utterly alone in my failure.*
> —Diary of Finn Christoffersen

Genevieve moved in with her aunt and uncle while Finn, with a thirty-five-dollar loan from Genevieve's uncle, returned to Butte to attempt to resurrect his former store. Unfortunately, the Depression had affected Butte even more than Seattle, and rebuilding his store was more difficult than Finn had hoped. He was lonely and wrote Genevieve daily, entreating her to bring the children and come and be with him, but only once did she answer his letters. She wrote,

> *Do not think to win me back until you are man enough to support your wife and children.*

Finn lived in the direst of circumstances, sending what little profit the store generated to Genevieve and the children. In the cold Montana winters he slept on the potatoes to keep them from spoiling. After eight months of loneliness he met a woman, the widow of the town's constable. She would come to the store daily, sometimes just to talk. Both were hungry for affection. They had an affair, and the woman became pregnant with Finn's child.

Around that same time Genevieve's aunt and uncle grew weary of their demanding niece and sent her back to Butte to be with her husband. When Genevieve learned of her husband's infidelity, she did what she could to punish him. She made him sleep at the store and would not allow him to eat with the family. During this time, Peter, now eight, and Thomas, seven, worked with their father at the store. As much as Finn begged for his wife's forgiveness, it never came.

> *I must wonder if I am to ever have Genny's love again. I have despaired of it. If I were a dog I would receive more affection.*
> —Diary of Finn Christoffersen

After several difficult years of Genevieve's cruel treatment, Finn, struggling with guilt, loneliness, and despair at not being able to adequately provide for his wife and family, decided that they all would be better off with the insurance money from his death. He shot himself in the head. His body was found by his oldest son, Peter.

Because Finn had committed suicide, his body was not allowed to be buried in the cemetery near his parents but was buried by Peter and a neighbor in a nearby wooded area. A wooden cross was constructed, but it has been lost to time and no one today knows for certain where my grandfather's body lies.

I set the book down, both disturbed and fascinated by what I had read. Like my great-grandfather, I had gone to Seattle to seek my fortune. And, when things turned, I had also considered taking my life. I now better understood my father's interest in discerning and recording this history. It was a way to understand himself. In a way, I had walked thousands of miles for the same reason.

I looked over at the clock. It was late, and it had already been a long day. I turned off the light, then lay back in my bed, my thoughts drifting from the past to the present and the future. I thought about Nicole asking about Falene. Then I thought about Falene and wondered what she'd been doing since she'd left me in St. Louis. Most of all, I wondered what McKale would think of it all and, if she were here, what she'd tell me to do. But that was nonsense. If she were here to tell me what to do, there would be no question of what to do.

"Why did you leave me, Mickey?" I said to the darkness. I closed my eyes and went to sleep.

CHAPTER

Nine

I now remember why I stopped playing chess
with my father. I feel less like a sparring
partner than a punching bag.

Alan Christoffersen's diary

The first thing my father said to me the next morning was, "I had a dream last night."

I sat down in the chair next to his bed, expecting him to tell me about it, but he didn't. I had brought with me my father's chess set, a heavy walnut inlaid board with carved wooden chessmen with felted bottoms.

"You brought my set," he said.

"The other one was too flimsy."

"Are you saying that's why you lost?"

"No, I take credit for that," I said. "Are you going to tell me about your dream?"

"It was about your mother," he said. "And McKale."

This piqued my interest even more. "Tell me about it."

"We were in this garden. It was big. Miles and miles of the most beautiful flowers and plants. It reminded me of the arboretum, but with more flowers. Thousands of them."

"Where McKale and I were married," I said.

"Right," he said. "It rained."

"It typhooned," I said.

He nodded. "We got wet. Anyway, in my dream, the girls were in this garden sitting on the bank of a brook. As I walked up to them they both looked up at me." My father paused, and his voice took on a faraway tone. "She was so beautiful. They both were. It was as if light was coming from their skin." He looked into my eyes. "It seemed so real."

"Did they say anything?"

"Your mother asked why I was there. She said I wasn't expected yet. Then—" He stopped abruptly.

"Then what?"

"Nothing," he said. "It was just a dream."

I looked at him curiously, wondering what he was holding back.

"Get out the chessboard," he said. "Time to take you to the woodshed."

"Really, you're trash-talking?"

I set up the chessboard on his table and pushed it toward him.

"You go first," he said.

"You're a gentleman," I said. I moved a pawn.

"You always move the same piece," he said.

"It works for me."

"What do you mean by *works*? You always lose."

"*Always* is a bit strong."

"When was the last time you won?"

"Never."

"Exactly."

"You should let me win sometime," I said.

"Then it wouldn't be winning."

After a few moves I said, "There were more offerings on the porch last night. They were from Pam and Margie."

He just nodded.

"Margie's gift was in the bushes. I think Pam threw it there."

"Pam's a determined woman," my father said. "She calls too frequently."

"How many women do you have chasing you?"

"I don't know."

"I'll bring their gifts tomorrow if you want. I'm sure there will be more by then."

"More baked goods?"

"Probably."

"You can have them."

"You liked the muffins," I said, looking at the empty basket.

"The nurses ate them," he said. "Have you heard from Nicole?"

"Not this morning. We had dinner last night."

He moved his knight. "Is she coming by today?"

"I think so. That's why she's here."

"She's a good girl."

"That's what you said yesterday."

"Probably still true." My father suddenly went quiet as he studied the board. We played for nearly five minutes without talking. Then he asked, "What's going to happen with her?"

"What do you mean?"

"You and her."

"I don't know. She asked me about Falene last night."

He looked up at me with concern. "What did she say?"

"She asked if I had found her. I told her I had, but I hadn't talked to her yet."

He went back to the board, taking my queen with his knight. "You need to be more careful," he said.

"Are you still talking about the game?"

"Yes. If you want advice about women, you could do better than me."

"So the dream you had. Did it make you wonder?"

"About what?"

"If some part of it was real."

I expected my father to dismiss the idea, but he didn't. "I think there might be more to heaven and earth than is dreamt of in my philosophy."

"You're softening about religion?"

"Religion? No. But God, that's a different matter. Never confuse the clock with the time."

"But you've changed your mind about God?"

"Maybe getting closer to the finish line does that to a man."

"What's with all the references to the end of life?" I said. "You're still young."

"Don't worry about it. It's the heart attack talking." He took another one of my pieces. "The other day I had this thought. If you look around, there's an order to things. The way the planets revolve around the sun is remarkably similar to the way electrons revolve around a nucleus. If science proves anything, it's that nothing comes from nothing. Something caused those things to act. It's not too hard to believe in the creator of that order. If you want to call that God, then maybe I do believe in God."

"What about an afterlife?"

"What about it?"

"Do you believe in one?"

"What you're really asking is, is there such a thing as a soul?" He looked over his move for a moment, then said, "It's hard to believe that there's nothing more to us than electrical impulses."

"Where do our souls go after death?"

Still looking at the board, he said, "Toledo."

I laughed. "Toledo?"

"Why not? It's as likely a destination as any."

We played a bit more in silence. As usual, I found myself in trouble.

"You're too impatient," he said. "You shouldn't move until you know it's right."

"Obviously I thought it was right."

"It wasn't," he said.

"I can see that now." I looked over the board. "I think I'm dead."

"You are."

"Speaking of dead, I read in your family history last night."

"That's an interesting segue. How far did you get?"

"I got to where your grandfather committed suicide."

He frowned. "Dead is right. It was tragic. Such unnecessary pain."

"Were you close to your grandmother?"

"No; I met her only once. At my mother's funeral. She was very old. I think she was just too mean to die. Or maybe it was her curse to see all her children die before her."

"Did you speak to her?"

"I told her that I was Peter's son. I thought it was pathetic that I had to tell my grandmother who I was. I still do."

"What did she say to that?"

"Nothing. She just grunted. Her selfishness carried its own punishment. She died alone. They found her body by the smell. They guessed she had already been dead for at least five days." He moved his queen. "Check."

I shook my head again.

"You're too impatient," he said again.

"It's my curse," I said. "Always has been."

"It's not a curse, it's a habit."

"Same thing," I said.

"Sometimes," he replied.

 ❧

My father took a nap around ten thirty. Nicole arrived a little before noon. My father was still sleeping, so we went down to the cafeteria for coffee. She asked how my father was, but for the most part she was quiet. She looked as if something was bothering her. I finally asked her what was wrong.

"Nothing."

"Want to talk about it?"

"No."

"If you change your mind, I'm here."

"I know."

An hour later, we returned to my father's room to find him awake. He looked especially happy to see Nicole.

"Hi, handsome," Nicole said. She leaned over his bed and they embraced. "How are you feeling today?"

"Like a million bucks," he said.

"Really?"

"Yeah. But a million bucks ain't what it used to be."

Nicole laughed. They talked for a long while. Twice I walked around the unit to stretch my legs. About six o'clock my father was getting sleepy again.

"You two run along," he said. "I'm going to rest a little. Or maybe a lot. Go to a movie or something."

"We're not going to a movie," Nicole said. "There's nothing I want to see."

"It doesn't matter what you watch, as long as it's more interesting than me."

"What could be more interesting than you?" She kissed him on the cheek. "Good night, Bob."

❧

As we walked out of the hospital I asked Nicole if she'd like to get some dinner.

"Thanks, but I think I'll just go back to the hotel."

I looked at her quizzically. "Are you sure? You've got to eat."

"I'm sure. Good night."

"Good night," I said. As I watched her walk to her car, I wondered what I had done.

I stopped at Vons grocery store on the way home and picked up a stack of TV dinners, some fruit and nuts, and a case of bottled water, something I never would have done had my father been home. (He couldn't understand why someone would pay for water when you could get it for free.)

When I got home there was a plate of sugar cookies on the doorstep. I heated up one of the dinners in the microwave, ate, then went to my room and continued reading from the family history.

II

Peter Christoffersen

My father, Peter, was a lanky, quiet child. Some called him withdrawn. He was known for having a fierce temper and was in more than a few fights with boys often much older and bigger than him. Considering the circumstances in which he was born, it's no surprise that he was of such a temperament. He was ten years old at the time of his father's death—old enough to recognize his mother's hand in it. To his dying day he never forgave her.

Nine weeks after Finn's death, Genevieve sold the store in Butte and, with the five thousand dollars she received from her husband's insurance, moved the family to Denver, Colorado. For a while, they lived a life of relative ease and prosperity. Peter took an apprenticeship with a local print shop setting type, but soon found he didn't have the patience for the work. For a time he also sold newspapers.

In 1941, when Peter was fifteen, Genevieve married a man named Winton Clark, a worker at the local Eaton Metal Products Company. Winton was a violent man who drank too much. He frequently beat Genevieve and the boys. One November night Winton came home late from work, drunk and belligerent. Finding his dinner cold, he began beating Genevieve. When Peter tried to intervene, Winton beat him so severely that his life was only spared by his mother's pleading.

Several hours later, after Winton had fallen asleep, Peter washed the blood from his face, packed a knapsack, said goodbye to his brother and sister, then struck Winton over the head with a heavy cast-iron skillet, emptied his pockets of $1.43, and left home for good.

Peter took a bus to a Denver army enlistment center, where he lied about his age and signed up to fight. The tide of the war was already turning as the Axis powers were stopped in Stalingrad and Midway. Peter was enrolled in the infantry and was eventually sent with the Allied troops to Utah Beach, where he saw the sand run red with blood and foam. His battalion pushed on to liberate France, then saw action in the Battle of the Bulge. He marched with the 99th Division in Moosburg as they freed the POWs. In his own words:

It was war, and I saw and did things that must change a man for the rest of his days.

Peter was honorably discharged thirty-six days after V-E Day (1945). He returned to Denver to see his brother and sister. His mother was still married to Winton, who had boasted that he'd beaten Peter "within an inch of his life" and vowed to "take him the final inch" should he ever "show his sorry face" in the home again. Unfortunately for Winton, Peter was now not only larger and stronger than him but battle hardened and trained in combat. He had killed men in war whom he had far less reason to dislike than Winton.

After taking a sound beating from Peter, Winton, who ironically was saved when Genevieve intervened, locked himself in his room and threated to call the police if Peter ever returned. The last thing Peter said to Genevieve was "Congratulations, Mother. You have found a man of your own quality."

Peter learned that his sister had married and moved to Pueblo, Colorado. His brother, Thomas, had also attempted to enlist in the army but, looking much younger than Peter, was rejected. Instead, he followed his grandfather's trade and went to work in the Kennecott Copper Mine in Bingham, Utah. In a cruel twist of irony, Thomas had been killed in a mining accident, thousands of miles away from the war.

Postwar America was a place of unbridled consumerism, and Peter got a good-paying job managing a downtown Denver appliance store, where he worked for several years. On October 17, 1947, at the age of twenty-one, he married Sara Krys White, a pretty waitress at the Rise'n Shine Diner, where he stopped every morning for coffee and pie. Sara baked her own wedding cake, and their wedding consisted of a brief ceremony held at the diner. That same day, Peter learned that his stepfather, Winton, had been killed in an automobile accident. Peter said it was the best wedding present he got.

He didn't attend his stepfather's funeral, though he later said he regretted not being there. "Not that I wished to pay my respects to the louse; rather, I wished to see the man in a state he most decidedly deserved."

I put the book down. I never knew my grandfather, but I could see how his temperament had influenced my father. Still, in many ways, my father was nothing like him. My dad had always been strict and serious of nature, but he wasn't violent. He had never spanked me and he rarely raised his voice. My father had done a lot to cultivate our family tree.

CHAPTER

Ten

My father is wiser than I've ever dared give
him credit for.

Alan Christoffersen's diary

The next morning my father was in the best mood he'd been in since I'd returned. I again cleared off his breakfast tray and set up the chess set.

"You got more cookies last night."

"From who?"

"I don't know. Does it matter?"

"I suppose not," he said.

"I also read more in the history."

"How far did you get?"

"To just before you're born."

"You're just getting to the good part," he said, smiling.

We started playing. A few moves in I asked, "Remember that time we went to that dude ranch in Wyoming?"

"Juanita Hot Springs. I mention it in the book."

"Was that your idea or Mom's?"

"Your mother's," he said. "I remember a horse almost ran away with you. You never liked horses after that."

"I didn't like them before," I said. "I like them less now."

He frowned. "Of course. McKale . . ."

"Did Mom know she had cancer then? During that trip?"

He nodded. "That's why we went on the trip. She wanted to create as many memories for you as she could." His voice became thoughtful. "You were the sun, moon, and stars to her. The last thing she said to me was 'Take care of our boy.'" He paused for a moment, then looked me in the eyes. "Did I?"

"Did you what?"

"Take care of you."

"Of course you did."

"I wonder sometimes. I didn't do the job that she would have. That wasn't going to happen. When we got married I warned her that I wasn't good with children."

"What did Mom say to that?"

"You know her, hope springs eternal . . ."

"No, I didn't know that about her."

"No, I guess you wouldn't. But she was the most hopeful person I have ever known. She said we'd just learn together. She told me that the most important things a parent could give a child were roots and wings. She said she'd provide the roots and I could teach you how to fly. I figured I could handle that part. I just didn't expect that she wouldn't be around." He frowned. "You spent most of your time with McKale anyway."

"Did that bother you?"

"No. I figured you needed the feminine interaction, and she filled the void."

"Did you ever think we would end up together?"

"No. Those things don't usually work out. But I thought it was good for you in the meantime." He went back to examining the board. "So what are you going to do with the rest of your life after your walk?"

"That's a good question," I said.

"Does it have a good answer?"

I looked up at him. "Lately I've been reconsidering things. I'm thinking that maybe I'll go to work in-house for an advertising agency. It doesn't have the growth potential of opening my own company, but it would be okay. I'd get the satisfaction of creativity without the pain of bill collecting or hassling with clients . . ."

"Or having someone steal your clients?" my father said. His gaze leveled on mine. "You're too talented to limit yourself, Al." He lifted one of the bishops he'd taken from me. "The past makes a good bishop but a poor king."

"What does that mean?" I said.

"It means that it's good to take counsel from the past but not to be ruled by it. Otherwise we end up using today to fight yesterday's battles and miss tomorrow's promise."

"That's pretty profound," I said.

"So what are you going to do with the rest of your life?"

"Stick around and find out."

"I'm planning on it."

Hearing him say that made me feel good.

"Is Nicole coming by today?" he asked.

"I don't know. I think being around me is hard on her."

"Maybe." He frowned. "Be good to her."

"Of course I will."

"Did you call Falene?"

"No."

"What are you waiting for?"

"I don't know."

"You'd better figure it out."

CHAPTER

Eleven

It's a shame that hearts don't come with manual overrides.

Alan Christoffersen's diary

My father was asleep when Nicole arrived at the hospital that afternoon. She looked as upset as she had the day before. "How is he?" she asked.

"Good," I said. Then I added, "He looks better than you do." She just kind of shrugged. "Do you want to talk?"

She slowly breathed out. "Okay."

We walked out of his room. The ICU waiting room wasn't crowded and we sat in a vacant corner.

"What's going on?" I asked.

She looked down for a moment, then slowly shook her head. "This is hard."

"I know how much he means—"

She looked up. "I don't mean your father, I mean us. Do you have any idea how hard it is to love someone who doesn't love you back?"

"I do love you."

"I don't mean like that," she said. "I don't know what I was thinking, coming here. I thought I could ignore my feelings, or that maybe they would just go away. But they're not." Tears welled up in her eyes. "They just get stronger. I love you too much to just be friends."

I didn't know what to say.

A tear rolled down her cheek. "Maybe I should just go home."

"Do you want to go home?"

She shook her head.

I took her hand. "I'm grateful that you're here. For both of us. But if it's too hard, I understand. So will my father."

For a moment she just sat there, wiping her eyes. Then she said softly, "I don't want to go."

"I don't want you to go," I said. "But I don't want to hurt you, either. I do love you."

"I know you do."

I kissed her forehead. Then I put my arms around her and held her. I felt like such an idiot. *Why didn't I love her?*

CHAPTER

Twelve

It's hard to believe that my mild-mannered accountant father was a warrior action figure.

Alan Christoffersen's diary

When Nicole had regained her composure I walked her to my father's room and left them alone. My heart ached for her, but I knew that her being with my father would help. He was good for her. They were good for each other.

After I got home I thought about what my father had said about calling Falene, but I couldn't do it. Especially not tonight. It felt like I would be throwing salt on Nicole's wounds. Instead I did some laundry, ate another one of my TV dinners, and lay down on my bed to read about my father.

III

Robert Alan Christoffersen

On June 16, 1953, Sara gave birth to her first and only child, Robert Alan Christoffersen. A week after my birth, my father lost his job after a scuffle involving the store owner's son. He took a brief stint as a bouncer at a bar, then found more steady work as a truck driver for the Vail Truck Line. His new profession provided a steady income, though it took him all across the country. He was home only three weekends a month.

I remember my mother as a lonely but dutiful wife and mother who devoted most of her time to raising me. On the weekends that Peter was home he drank heavily, and Mom waited on him hand and foot, eager to please him.

I never really knew my father. It seemed he had little interest in me. I learned, at a young age, that if I asked him about the war, he was eager to talk, so I would think up questions to ask him.

Though my father was often harsh and aloof, he was not abusive. The only time he ever struck me I likely deserved it, as I was a teenager and I had taken some money from his wallet without asking.

The money he made driving was sufficient for our needs, and I never felt deprived like some of the other children in our neighborhood did. During the summer of my fourteenth birthday, we moved to a better neighborhood in the suburban area of Lakewood. I attended Lakewood High School, where I played forward on the school's varsity basketball team. My senior year I played on the team that placed third in state, the farthest our school had ever progressed in the tournament.

I had always been a little shy around the opposite sex, but, beginning in my sophomore year of high school, I dated several girls. My first real girlfriend was Jodi Reynolds. She was a pretty blond girl and was the first attendant at the sophomore "sock hop" prom. Then, halfway through my junior year, I fell in love with a girl named Kate Mitchell, a beautiful brunette who looked a little like a combination of a young Audrey Hepburn and Annette Funicello. We got along well, and my heart was broken that summer when her father took a job in Phoenix and she moved out of state with her family. We wrote for a few months, but once September came we both found ourselves swept into life at school and eventually met others.

During these years, it was important to my father that

I work. I had a job at a hot dog stand called Der Wiener-schnitzel, and then at Peck & Shaw, a used car dealership where I detailed cars before they went on the lot to be sold. It was a volatile time in the world, a time of social unrest and protests, much of it over the war in Vietnam. In 1969, during my junior year, the first draft lottery since World War II was initiated. A year later, four students were killed in a protest at Kent State University in Kent, Ohio. My father was a vocal critic of "the hippies," and the back window of our station wagon bore a decal that read:

AMERICA.
LOVE IT OR LEAVE IT.

I suppose that was why I offered no resistance when my draft notice arrived a week after my high school graduation in June 1971. While some of my high school friends were burning their draft cards or relocating to Canada, I reported to basic training in Fort Lewis, just south of the Seattle-Tacoma area of Washington, not far from where my grandfather had lived during the Depression.

The transformation from civilian to soldier is a fascinating, if not painful process. On the first day everyone arrives with the accoutrements of their own class and social caste. The military is the great equalizer. At the end of the day, we all had the same haircut, our clothing was the same, and our status was equally lowly. Our pay matched our status: we were paid seventy-five dollars a month to risk our lives. For some it was the most money they had ever seen.

During my sixth week in basic training I was called in by my sergeant and told that my father had died. I was in shock. I was told that I could take a hardship leave, but it would have meant starting all over again with a different group. At that moment I realized that I had, in part, gone into the war to win my father's approval. Now he was gone. I called my mother, and she agreed I should stay.

After eight weeks we were given our MOS—military occupational specialty. This is when each of us should have received an assignment that matched our individual skill set, but at that point in the war they were sending everyone they could to infantry. One member of our group raised his hand and said he spoke Chinese. The captain said, "We don't care, soldier. We need bodies."

They needed soldiers in the jungle. I was classified 11B. The B stands for "Bravo," but the veterans just say it stands for "bush." There was no way around it: we were all going to see combat, up close and personal.

From basic training we were sent to AIT—advanced infantry training. Jungle training. Same discipline and drilling as basic training, but more classes. We had to take apart our rifles and put them back together in sixty seconds—blindfolded. We learned how to throw grenades, dig foxholes, fire and service a .50-caliber machine gun, and set up ambushes or establish a perimeter with M18 Claymore mines. Most of all, we learned how to move as a platoon.

After we completed AIT we were given another test. I must have scored high, because that afternoon a colonel called me in and told me he thought I was NCO (noncommissioned officer) material. He told me I'd make more money and get to lead some people. I said it sounded good to me. He wanted to send me to Fort Benning in Georgia for NCO school but first wanted me to extend my service a year.

I had no desire to make the military my life, so I said no to the extension. They sent me to NCO school anyway. I guess they were short on leaders. NCO school lasted a couple of months, and although I'd only been in the military for a total of five months, I came out the same rank as my drill sergeant, who had served for six years.

During our second week in NCO our orders came to report to Fort Carson in preparation for being sent to Vietnam. Fort Carson is located near Colorado Springs, just a couple of hours from my home in Denver.

As I prepared to go, I was presented with another opportunity. I was called in and asked to go to OCS (officer candidate school) at Fort Benning. Again I was asked to extend my time in the army, and again I turned them down. Again, they sent me anyway.

In OCS I was trained to lead. I learned how to read maps and was taught communication and leadership skills. I would graduate as a second lieutenant—the rank of a platoon leader—and I would be calling the shots in the bush. I was in OCS for fourteen weeks, and at the end of the training I was sent back to Colorado to await my combat orders.

While I was there I saw my mother twice. She was handling the death of my father better than I had expected. She told me that my father had been gone so much that a part of her just felt he was still out on the road.

The second time I went to see her was two days before I was to fly to Vietnam. The reality that it might be the last time she saw her son was difficult for her to bear. She broke down as I started to go and she told me to "be careful," which was like telling a surfer not to get wet. I told her that I would do my best.

On February 7, 1972, about two hundred of us were sent by military transport from Denver to San Diego, where we boarded a TWA airliner to fly to Vietnam. We were flown into the base at Long Binh, about thirty-three kilometers from Saigon. Long Binh was the largest US Army base in Vietnam, with more than fifty thousand men and women.

We arrived at night, and after we landed the lights in the airport and on the plane were all turned off, keeping us from being an easy target for mortars and rockets.

I'll never forget stepping from the plane. Even at night the hot, wet air hit me like a blast furnace. I had never before experienced such humidity. Or such uncertainty. I briefly wondered what my father would think of where I was, or if I felt the same emotions he had on D-Day, but I quickly dismissed the thoughts. My father's opinions had become irrelevant—not just because of his death, but because my new circumstances demanded it.

Just as oppressive as the humidity was the country's smell. The jungle is thick and wet, a massive, living compost that fills the air with heat and the stench of decay.

We were immediately taken to bunkers to sleep. That night we came under mortar and rocket fire, and most of us newbies stayed up expecting an attack until one of the MPs asked us why we weren't sleeping. When we told him he laughed. He said this was just the Vietcong welcoming us to Nam.

Early the next morning we were rushed out onto a large, fenced-in field to be given our assignments. An officer with a bullhorn addressed us with a greeting I'll never forget.

He said, "Welcome to Vietnam. This will likely be the most interesting year of your life. Some of you will go home. Some of you won't. Try to be one of those who goes home."

Then he walked around shouting out our assignments. The parceling took about an hour. I didn't have to wait long before he shouted, "Christoffersen, First Cavalry."

The 1st Cavalry was an air-mobile unit, meaning we were flown into combat by helicopters. As we walked to our assignments, we passed soldiers going home. They were on the other side of a chain-link fence, and most of them were pretty ragged looking. One of the soldiers came up next to the fence and waved us over. "Hey, newbies."

Me and two others walked up to him.

"If I were you," he said, "I'd kill myself right now."

The first month in the jungle is the most critical for survival, because you don't know what you don't know. I was there to take over for a platoon leader who had just three weeks left. I had to learn fast. I was fortunate to have a new best friend, a Chinese-Cambodian man named Tac Fuhn. He was what the army called a Kit Carson Scout, but he was really just a mercenary and was paid for every VC we killed. I asked him why he worked for us instead of the North Vietnamese. He replied, "The Americans pay more." Every day I was glad he was on our side.

My first firefight came after two weeks in the bush. We walked into a clearing and saw four VC in their black pajama-like uniforms. Both sides were equally surprised, and we both fired. I shot off about thirty rounds. I told Fuhn that I thought I got one of them. He laughed and said, "Only if he was hanging from the top of the tree."

I had wondered if, when the time came, I would be able to shoot another man. I discovered that, when someone's shooting at you, it's pretty easy to shoot back. I was fortunate that my first encounter with the enemy was just a few VC and not an ambush with a dug-in army.

Pasted in the book was a picture of my father I had never seen before. He was fifteen years younger in the picture than I was now. This was not an image of the staid accountant I knew. My father was an action figure.

I spent the next ten months in the bush. We became soldiers. Tough. Confident. Skilled. We learned to remain calm under fire. My biggest fear wasn't death, it was being captured or, worse, losing one of my men. I have heard that new mothers have dreams about losing their babies. Sometimes I had dreams about losing one of my men. There's a bonding that takes place that only someone under such duress can understand.

Everyone had a nickname: Val, Slim, Abe, Sparky, Willyboy, Wailin' Wagers, Forkey, and Flash. My men just called me L.T. or Lieutenant, though after a few months some took to calling me Lucky, since I never got hit in battle.

In some ways, I knew my men better than their own mothers knew them; when a man faces mortality, you see who he really is. I learned that, in the face of death, these men I commanded would come through for me. I loved them, and I discovered that I worried about them more than I worried about myself. I'm proud to say that I only lost one of them, though by the end of my deployment, most of them had been wounded.

The Vietnamese were deadly opponents, and every firefight reminded us of that. The VC created remarkable underground bunker complexes. I remember Tac Fuhn saying to me, "We are close to a bunker." I said, "Where?" He pointed to the ground and said, "We are standing on it. See the airhole?"

There is one firefight that stands out to me more than the others. We had stumbled upon a huge VC complex. We were extremely outnumbered and taking a lot of fire. I called in a B-52 strike. By the time the planes arrived, most of the enemy had scattered into the jungle, disappearing like sand through our fingers.

Following a major firefight we were required to report a body count, so after the ground was secure and our wounded cared for, we patrolled the compound for dead VC. There was one casualty I'll never forget. As I approached the still body of a dead soldier I found that she was a woman and pregnant. Her eyes were wide open, and her hand was on her stomach. There were two bullets through her throat, one through her forehead, and one through her abdomen. I don't know what she was doing in combat, but she had been carrying a gun, which made her a justifiable target.

Justifiable or not, I dreamed about the woman many times. Her wide, lifeless eyes would suddenly blink and she would stare at me, her face distorted with fear and hatred. Then she would ask, "Why?"

The environment itself seemed to be our enemy. I arrived in Nam during the monsoon season, and coming from Colorado I had never seen anything like it. Rain would fall, uninterrupted, for weeks on end. We were always wet. We didn't wear socks, as they would only cause fungus to grow. There were times we went more than a week without being dry.

There were also snakes. There was a particularly nasty little green pit viper, with bright red eyes, that hung from trees. They were hard to see and I had a few snap at me as I brushed by. They posed enough of a danger that our medics carried antivenom for them. One of our guys was bit, and even with the antivenom it was several days before he was himself again.

Maybe the most annoying of Nam's creatures were the leeches. One morning one of my men woke with a leech on his eyelid. By the time we got it off, his eye was pretty messed up. We wore leech garters to keep them from climbing up to the soft tissue of our crotches.

IV

Coming Home

I had been in the jungle for nearly ten months when our platoon was engaged in our largest firefight. Twenty-two of my thirty men were injured and had to be medevaced out. With most of my men out of commission, I was brought back with them to Long Binh. I assumed I would be given a new platoon, something I wasn't happy about.

While waiting for my orders in Long Binh, I was informed by my commander that my request for an early release to attend college had been granted. I was done. The war was over for me. Two days later it was me walking on the other side of the fence watching as frightened newbies lined up to take their assignments. As the plane lifted, everyone on board spontaneously broke into applause.

We flew into the Oakland airport, and I kissed the tarmac as I got off. We were taken to a big hangar to be processed out. It took three days for me to be released.

I was still in my uniform as I flew from Oakland to Denver. I didn't see what some returning Vietnam veterans reported—angry, jeering crowds calling us "baby killers" or spitting on us. I'm not saying it didn't happen, it just didn't happen to me. My mother met me at the airport. It had been only eleven months since she'd sent me off from Fort Carson, but it felt like a lifetime. She had changed a lot since I'd seen her last. She had aged. Her hair was completely gray, and she seemed weary.

Just two weeks later I was a student at the University of Colorado in Boulder, wearing bell-bottom jeans and a polyester disco shirt. Reentry into civilian life had its challenges, but having been in Vietnam gave my life context. I remember talking to a fellow student who was upset about our upcoming final. He said to me, "Why are you so calm? It's half our grade!" I replied, "Because even if we fail, we'll still be alive in the morning."

Vietnam was the most controversial of conflicts, and even with my rank and decorations, I wondered if my father would have been proud of me. I discovered that there was a smugness to many of the older vets. Some of them seemed to believe that what they had done mattered and what we had done didn't. No matter the rightness of the cause, we, like them, answered the call of our country. We felt the same fear, the same pain, and faced the same risks. But, unlike them, we came back not to ticker tape parades and celebrations but to a largely indifferent and ungrateful nation.

Walking on Water

We had put our lives on the line for a war that had initially been popularly ratified by both the politicians and the people. We had risked our lives for *their* decisions, not ours, yet they hated us for it. But no matter the country's schizophrenia, to me the war was more than a news story. It was a part of my life. And though it all seemed to have passed by like a dream, sometimes, in those dreams, I would still see the pregnant Vietnamese woman, her neck and forehead pierced, her dark eyes open, staring at me. And each time she would ask, "Why?"

CHAPTER

Thirteen

Wandering through just one paragraph of my father's history has changed Key West for me more than walking a few thousand miles.

Alan Christoffersen's diary

Why didn't I know any of this about my father?

∽

It was past midnight when I set down the book. I suppose we as children are selfish by nature, judging our parents in the context not of *their* worlds and challenges but of *our* worlds and how they meet our needs. Even as we mature we rarely think of them as having been young like us.

Reading about my father, more than a decade younger than I was right now, leading a group of men through a murderous jungle, cast him in a different light. He was stronger and more courageous than I had ever given him credit for. He was better than me.

Of course I knew that my father had served in the war, but I'd never given it much thought. I certainly had never understood it from his perspective. The only time we had spoken about Vietnam was when my eighth-grade history class was studying the war and I asked my father if he knew anything about it—which was like asking the pope if he knew anything about Catholicism. Outside of that discussion, he never spoke of it. I didn't think he was traumatized by the experience, but rather that he had moved past it, and chose not to be defined by it any more than any other experience in his life. Perhaps it had made him more serious, but, considering his father, I think he would have been a serious person whether he served in the war or not.

I think the war might have affected him in another profound way. It taught him the true and temporary nature of all things—that nothing remains the same forever. Perhaps that's what got him through my mother's death.

∾

I arrived at the hospital the next morning eager to talk to my father about what I had read, but he was asleep when I got there. I sat there for nearly an hour, reading, before he woke.

"What time is it?" he asked.

His voice startled me. "It's nearly ten."

"I slept in," he said in a deep voice. "I didn't sleep well last night."

"I'm sorry. Do you want some breakfast?"

He didn't answer immediately, but looked around the room. "Maybe in a little while."

"I read pretty late last night," I said.

"What did you read about?"

"You. Your childhood. Vietnam."

"Nam," he said, as if he were speaking of a person. "That was an interesting time."

"Interesting or terrifying?"

"Both," he said. Then, surprisingly, he suddenly grinned.

"What's that for?" I asked.

He looked back up at me. "I just remembered something funny."

"In Vietnam?"

"I'm sure even hell has its occasional humor," he said. "This one time after we'd been in the bush for six weeks

---

9 7

they flew us to Long Binh for some R and R. When we landed I was told that we were going to be inspected by a new general, and I wasn't real happy about that. After fighting in the jungle for more than a month, the last thing I wanted was some starched stateside general casting judgment on us.

"As he looked us over he focused his attention on this one guy, Private Forkey, who was standing kind of slumped. Forkey was regular military. He'd been in the army for eighteen years and was still a private. He'd been promoted to sergeant twice before, but both times was busted back down for insubordination." My father grinned at me. "Forkey had trouble with authority. The general shouted, 'Soldier, stand up straight and show some respect.' Forkey looked the general in the eye and said, 'What are you going to do? Send me to Vietnam?'

"Even though we tried to keep straight faces, we all burst out laughing. Fortunately, it turned out the general was a regular guy after all, and he said, 'I guess you have a point there.'" My father shook his head. "It was a crazy time. I had these two kids in my platoon from South Chicago. We called them the Polaski brothers, which was funny because they weren't named Polaski and they weren't brothers. They were both Polish and had come over together. Those boys were fearless. They had belonged to a gang on the tough Chicago streets and were what we called 'two or ten.' That means they'd been arrested and the judge gave them an option, two years in Vietnam or ten years in prison." My father smiled. "Most of their conversations were about how they would get a mortar back to South Chicago. They eventually devised a plan to bring one over piece by piece."

"Did they ever do it?" I asked.

"Probably not," he said. "You would have heard about it on the news if they did. I think it was just an idea to keep their minds occupied." His eyes grew serious. "In moments of crisis, you do what you need to do to survive. Mentally and physically. You'd be surprised what the mind is capable of."

"You're a strong man," I said.

"So are you," he replied. He settled back a little in his bed. "So you and Nicole had a talk yesterday."

"She told you?"

He nodded. "Breaks my heart. She's a sweet girl. You're sure you're not in love with her?"

"It would be convenient."

"Love is rarely convenient," he replied. "You still haven't called Falene?"

"No. Not yet." Before he could ask why, I changed the subject. "How are you feeling?"

"I'm still here."

"That's a good thing."

"That depends on which alternative destination you're thinking of," he replied.

"Want to play some chess?"

He breathed out slowly. "No. Not today. Maybe I'll read."

"Can I get you something?"

"I could use one of the newsmagazines. I feel like I've lost touch with the world."

"I'll find you one," I said.

I went downstairs to the gift shop and purchased copies of both *Newsweek* and *Time*. When I returned to my father's room he was asleep again. I read the magazines while I waited for him to wake, but after an hour he was still snoring.

I left the magazines next to his bed and went out to the nurses' station to see if Dr. Witt was in. A nurse told me that he would be in around one. I checked on my father again, then went out and got some lunch, then went to a bookstore and picked up a couple of thriller novels, then went back to the hospital. When I walked into the room my father was sitting up and reading *Time*. "Thanks for getting these."

"You're welcome," I said. "Have you heard from Nicole?"

"She said she'd be here around three."

"Maybe I'll leave before she gets here."

"That might be better," he said.

It was already a few minutes past two, so I said goodbye and went out to find Dr. Witt. He was in the hall, and he looked up at me as I approached. "Alan, right?"

I was surprised that he remembered my name. "Yes. I wanted to ask how my father's doing."

We stepped to the side of the hall. "He's stable, but I'm not seeing the progress I had hoped for. His heart still isn't pumping effectively on its own, so he still requires medication and close monitoring."

"What do we do?"

"Just what we're doing. Wait."

"Wait for what?"

"Change."

❦

I was feeling restless, so on the way home I stopped by a gym where I purchased a temporary membership along with some gym shorts and a T-shirt. I lifted weights and rode a stationary bike until I was soaked with sweat. Then I went back to the house and showered.

After working out I wasn't very hungry, so I had just a bowl of Cheerios, then went to my room and went back to reading.

V

Kate

I went to the University of Colorado for three reasons: First, tuition was, at the time, relatively cheap; second, there was work available in the area; and third, they had a decent accounting program.

One October evening I was having a beer with some classmates at a restaurant-bar called The Sink when a beautiful young woman walked in. One of my buddies stood to talk to her, and I realized she was Kate Mitchell, my high school sweetheart who had moved to Phoenix. Kate seemed as happy to see me as I was her, and we spent the rest of the evening catching up on our lives since we'd last seen each other. That evening I walked her back to her dorm and we ended up talking until the sun came up. I was smitten. Or re-smitten. After that we spent every possible moment together.

A week before Christmas break, William Guest, one of my comrades from Nam (aka Willy-boy), called to say he was getting married on December 18 and asked me to be his best man. He lived south of Miami in Florida City. I invited Kate to accompany me to Florida and she accepted. We flew into Miami, and William and his soon-to-be bride, Sally, picked us up at the airport. We stayed at William's parents' house. The morning after the wedding we borrowed Sally's car and drove two and a half hours south to Key West for the day.

It was a beautiful day, a far cry from Denver's snow and subfreezing temperatures. We ate conch fritters and key lime pie and visited some of Ernest Hemingway's haunts, like Sloppy Joe's Bar and his home on Whitehead Street, which had been turned into a bookstore.

At sunset we sat on a small strip of beach near the southernmost tip of the island. I rolled up my pant legs, walked out into the water, and found a shell. I brought it back and gave it to Kate and asked her to marry me. I don't know if she was completely sure I was serious, but she said yes. She might be the first girl ever to be proposed to with a seashell.

Later that night, we called our parents and told them our news. Kate's parents were happy. So was my mother, who had always liked Kate. When we got back to Denver I bought Kate a real ring and we picked a date in June to get married.

We spent Christmas Eve and morning in Denver with my mother, then flew to Phoenix and stayed with Kate's family until New Year's Day. Her family treated me really well, even though Kate's father was recovering from surgery. He suffered from severe diabetes, and the surgeons had just amputated most of his toes. I wondered if it might be his last Christmas, which, unfortunately, it was. He lived to see us married, though. We were married on June 28 at the Brotherhood of Man Desert Chapel in Scottsdale, Arizona.

I graduated with my BS on December 13, 1976, with a major in accounting. It was my great fortune that I graduated with a job. Twelve weeks before graduation I went to an on-campus interview with Peat Marwick of Denver, one of the big eight accounting firms. Back then you didn't need to complete a master's program to be a CPA, and I was hired on the spot as a staff monitor.

After graduation, Kate and I moved to Thornton, Colorado, a pleasant, growing suburb just ten miles northeast of Denver. The next week I reported for work in the auditing division on the twenty-first floor of the Peat Marwick building in downtown Denver.

I was given eighteen months to get my accounting certificate. I took my CPA exam and passed four of the five sections on my first attempt. I went back three months later and finished. I received my certificate after I'd been there for six months. Unfortunately there wasn't much time for celebrating. Kate's father died two days later.

I lay back in bed, my head swimming with these revelations. Not only had my parents been to Key West but they were engaged there. Why hadn't my father told me? How could he have kept something that *important* from me?

CHAPTER

Fourteen

What I read in my father's book tonight was difficult. It was like watching a rerun of a show I hated the first time.

Alan Christoffersen's diary

The next morning my father was eating breakfast as I walked into his room. I was less than subtle. "Why didn't you tell me that Key West was such a significant place for you? You didn't even tell me that you'd been there."

He looked up at me for a moment, then said, "You didn't ask."

I shook my head. "No, that's not a good enough answer."

He saw how upset I was and set down his fork. "No. You're right." He looked at me, waiting for me to calm a little. "When I heard you were walking to Key West, I wanted to say something. But I knew I shouldn't. It was a difficult time for you, and this was your journey, not mine. Key West means something entirely different to you than it does to me. As far as I'm concerned, it's not even the same place. That's why I didn't tell you."

My anger dissipated. "I'm sorry. You're right."

"There's more," he said. "I had planned on being in Key West when you arrived. But seeing how things have gone south for me, I'm not sure that's going to happen." He must have read the concern in my face because he quickly added, "I'm not saying I won't be there, but just in case I'm not, I want you to do something for me."

"What?"

"In the nightstand next to my bed there's a yellow envelope with your name on it. I want you to take it with you to Key West. Will you do that for me?"

"What's in the envelope?"

"You'll see when you get there." He looked me in the eye. "You'll do it?"

"Of course, but only if you're not there."

He forced a smile. "I hope I'll be there."

I sat down next to him. "I'm sorry I came blustering in here like that."

"It's okay," he said. "You're entitled to your feelings."

"How are you feeling today?"

"Same old."

"Have you talked to Dr. Witt lately?"

He frowned. "Yes. I don't think things are going the way he was hoping they would."

"Why do you say that?"

"I asked him when I could go home. He said it might be a while. Either that or he's trying to keep Nicole around."

"Nicole?"

"He's got his eye on her. He's asked me about her a few times. And he lights up like a Christmas tree whenever she's around."

This was news. "Really? Has Nicole noticed?"

"I don't know."

I didn't know what to say. I felt funny about it.

My dad's eyebrows fell. "You're not jealous, are you?"

"Of course not."

"Are you sure?"

"I don't know."

"You don't have a right to be," he said.

"I know."

"Besides, it's a good thing."

"Why do you say that?"

"I get more attention from the doctor this way."

⚬

I saw Nicole briefly that afternoon. Changing of the guard. She didn't look as upset as she had the last time I'd seen her. "You okay?" I asked.

"I'm okay," she said softly. She touched my arm. "Thank you for being so sweet to me the other day. I know it's hard for you too."

"You're my friend," I said. "Maybe my only friend."

She hugged me. "How's your dad today?"

"I don't know. He said he's not feeling any better."

Nicole nodded as if she already knew. "It may take time," she said. "Time heals all wounds."

"I'm counting on that."

"Have a good night," she said. "I'll see you tomorrow."

⚬

The first thing I did when I got home was look in my father's nightstand for the envelope he'd told me about. It was there near the front, a standard number 10 envelope made of bright yellow paper. The envelope contained more than just a letter. It bulged at one end. I put it back in the nightstand.

It had been nearly a week since I'd done any walking, so I put on my gym shorts and shirt and went for a long walk, passing the arboretum where McKale and I had gotten married. It felt good to see the old places and relive the memories they brought back. It also felt good to get out on the road again. I find that I can think better when my legs are moving.

I walked for nearly three hours, returning just as the sun had begun to fall. Then I took my dad's car to the store and bought some more groceries. I broiled a steak, which I ate with an arugula salad.

After I finished eating I cleaned up the kitchen, took a shower, then went to my room for the evening, ready to get back to my reading. The next chapter held special interest. It was about me.

VI

A Son

In October of the following year, Kate informed me that she was pregnant. I was as excited as I was terrified. I worried about what kind of father I would be. I didn't exactly have a sterling role model. I thought I could approach fatherhood the way I had approached survival in the jungle of Vietnam: I'd figure it out as I went. The difference was, I had more training for war.

Being a mother was natural for Kate. In fact, it was as if she had come into herself. My son, Alan Christoffersen, was born June 5, 1979. He weighed eight pounds and one ounce and was twenty-one inches long. Kate wanted to name him after me, but I didn't think Bob would be a popular name in the future, so we used my middle name, Alan. He was a beautiful boy. He was healthy with a strong pair of lungs and a head full of hair. In his birth I discovered a paternal side of me that I didn't know existed. I became fiercely protective.

Kate was as smitten with her son as any mother has ever

been. She called our boy "mister" and "little dreamy." Alan was a smart kid and inventive, and showed an early interest and talent in art. At the age of three, he was drawing pictures of animals and people. He was also a very handsome boy, and every year his grade school teacher would inform us that the girls in his class all had crushes on him.

As much as I loved him, there were times I felt awkward about my inability to emotionally connect with my son. Fortunately his mother more than made up for it.

With the exception of the death of Kate's mother, the next eight years of our life were idyllic. I continued to climb the ladder at Peat Marwick while Kate raised our son and made our house a home. On June 9, 1987—everything changed.

•   •   •

It was early on a Wednesday morning. I was shaving in the bathroom and Kate was in the shower when she found a lump in her breast. We were both concerned, but she continued her morning ritual of getting Alan off to school. She promised she would call her doctor that day.

That afternoon she called me at work to tell me that her doctor had taken her right in and scheduled a biopsy. Two days later the biopsy came back as malignant, and her doctor made an appointment for her with a cancer specialist, Dr. Mark Haroldsen, whom we saw just three days later. To our relief, he told us that he believed we had caught the cancer early, but we needed an MRI to confirm his diagnosis, which we got immediately.

The results came back that same week. The tumor was larger than Dr. Haroldsen thought. Also, the surrounding tissue was all precancerous, so Kate would need a mastectomy. As bad as the news was, there was more. Dr. Haroldsen pointed out a dark shadow under Kate's arm requiring a second biopsy, this one of Kate's lymph nodes.

That evening we sat Alan down and told him that his mother was sick. As usual he was very inquisitive and wanted to know what a tumor was. When we finally used the word *cancer* he began to cry. He told us that one of his classmates' fathers had died of cancer that year. Kate just held him and told him not to worry. She said, "Don't worry, little man. Your mama's not going anywhere."

I had slept in the jungle drenched by monsoon rains and lying in mud two inches thick within a hundred yards of the VC, but I didn't sleep at all that night.

My mind was flooded with painful memories. I remembered the talk. It was after dinner, and my mother, father, and I were in the living room. I knew something was very wrong. Children sense these things. I was sitting cross-legged on the red and green couch. The amber curtains with their odd, Nazca-like designs were drawn for the night. The gilded macaroni art I had made at school hung on the wall. I remembered the musky scent of my father's Old Spice and the pattern of tiny red diamonds on his navy blue tie. Most of all I remembered the look of fear in his eyes.

I continued reading.

Two days later the results came back from the second biopsy. The cancer had spread to the lymph nodes. The operation was changed to a mastectomy with a full lymph node removal. Just one week later Kate had the operation. It was another very long week before we got the results.

The cancer was even worse than previously thought. Much worse. It had spread to other parts of Kate's body, including her lungs. Dr. Haroldsen said that, as it was, Kate likely had less than six months to live, but, with heavy chemotherapy, we could buy a few more months. I broke down crying. Kate squeezed my hand tightly, and tears also filled her eyes. But I honestly don't think they were for her. All she said was "Oh, my little Alan . . ."

I had to pause a moment, as my eyes had filled with tears.

Kate became determined to make the most of the time she had left. Over the next twelve weeks we took a trip to Juanita Hot Springs, a dude ranch in Wyoming, with a stop in Yellowstone National Park. She went home to her family in Arizona twice (with Alan; she was always with Alan) and we visited Bryce Canyon in southern Utah.

Though sometimes it was practically all she could do to get out of bed, she made that Christmas magical. We saw plays and attended concerts. She baked Christmas cookies and even frosted Pop-Tarts with Christmas holly. It was a season of the most incredible love and beauty and denial.

The new year slapped us back to reality. Kate spent most of her time in bed. On January 12 she decided to stop the chemo. The next day we had the most difficult talk of our lives with Alan. Kate told him that she wasn't going to get better. Alan cried, but he didn't break down. A change in him had already begun. I had noticed that he was more serious. He rarely laughed anymore.

Over the next weeks he missed a lot of school to be with his mother. Kate read dozens of books to him, but mostly they just talked and talked. There were good and bad days, but each new week brought more of the latter as her condition worsened.

On the night of February 13, Alan made her a Valentine's Day card and left it at the side of her bed. She never saw it. She never woke up again.

It was as if I was reliving it all. I set the book down and wept.

CHAPTER

Fifteen

I suppose that to be a parent is to be misunderstood. Perhaps this is the greatest evidence of parental love.

Alan Christoffersen's diary

I had a fitful night. I dreamed of my mother's death over and over. I dreamed of seeing her dead, her still, lifeless body growing cold. I woke sweating and tangled in my sheets. And then I would fall asleep and dream it again—only sometimes it was McKale I saw.

The next morning my father knew I was in pain as soon as I walked into his room. I suppose it was written across my face.

"You read about your mother, didn't you?"

I sat down, my fingers knit together between my knees. "Yes, sir."

"Those were hard days," he said softly. He looked at me with sadness. "Hard, horrible days. I'm sorry you had to go through them at such a young age."

I looked up at my father and wondered if I was about to go through horrible days again.

❧

The next week passed in a haze. Though I came to the hospital every day, my father slept most of the time. When he was awake we didn't talk any more about the family history. I had stopped reading, preferring instead to anesthetize my brain with whatever was on television that night.

Things weren't going well. It was becoming more and more clear that my father wasn't getting better. I had been back in California for thirteen days when my father said gravely, "Al, we need to talk."

"About what?" I asked.

"My affairs."

I was about to protest when he weakly raised his hand. "I'm not giving up the ghost. But I'm going to die sometime, so we might as well prepare for it. You'll be grateful later. I've handled more inheritance and probate problems than I care to remember. It's better to take care of things in advance." I must have still looked distressed, because he added, "It will make me feel a lot better to get this off my chest."

I felt like that little boy again sitting cross-legged on the sofa. "All right."

"You need to find something to write on."

There was a notepad by the phone. I picked it up.

"No, you need something substantial. I'm sure there's a shop somewhere in the hospital. Go buy a steno pad and pen."

"All right," I said.

I took the elevator down to the lobby. The gift shop was right next to the entryway. It had arched French glass windows with cream trim and racks of flowers for sale near the front door. I purchased a yellow notepad and a mechanical pencil. I'm not sure why, but I also bought a bright bouquet of pink, yellow, and orange gerbera daisies. I had never bought flowers for my father before.

When I got back to the room my father was lying still with his eyes closed.

"I'm back," I said. I set the flowers down on the windowsill.

He opened his eyes, then gestured to the flowers. "What are those for?"

"They're flowers. What do you think they're for?"

"Save them for my funeral," he said. "No, scratch that. I don't want flowers. I want donations made to the American Red Cross."

I sat down in the chair next to his bed. "We're not talking about your funeral."

"Of course we are. Write that down," he said. "No flowers."

I took the notepad and flipped it open. "All right, no flowers . . ."

"Instead of flowers, I want donations made to the American Red Cross or the American Cancer Society. Make sure you provide an address or contact phone number on the obituary, or they won't do it. They'll intend to, but they won't get around to it."

I scrawled his directions.

"Designate a page just for my funeral," he said. "Write it down on the top."

I looked up at him. "Dad, this . . ."

"*This* is no time to be squeamish. I just had a major heart attack. My heart could stop at any moment. Let's get this over with."

Knowing that he wouldn't bend, I wrote *Funeral Directions* at the top of the first page.

"I've already purchased the plot next to Mom in the Elysium Gardens Cemetery in Denver. I want to be buried next to her. I've made arrangements with Beard Mortuary to handle everything. Write that down."

"Beard Mortuary? How do you spell it?"

"Just like the facial hair. 555-0121. It's a Pasadena number."

I wrote down the number.

"Did you get it?"

"Yes, sir."

"Just tell them you're calling regarding Bob Christof-fersen. Everything is paid for. I purchased one of those pre-need plans. There will be a memorial service at their little chapel, then the casket will be shipped to Colorado for burial. You won't need a headstone; I bought one of those couple stones when Mom died. They just need to engrave the final date on my side. Beard will take care of that as well." He looked up at me. "You got all that?"

"Yes, sir."

"Start another page. Head it *Miscellaneous*."

I wrote it down.

"After I die, you'll have to cancel things. Cable, Internet, newspaper, magazine subscriptions. There are at least a dozen things you'll need to shut down. I keep the automatic monthly charges on the blue Visa card. Once you cancel that, it will put everyone on notice. There's a list of everything with my final instructions inside the top drawer of my desk—the long, thin drawer, not the one on the side. I put the Visa card in an envelope next to the list."

"When did you do all this?" I asked.

"Two years ago," he said. "I'm an accountant. I do this for people all the time."

I wrote on my pad.

"My password is TacFuhn72. It's spelled T-A-C-F-U-H-N."

I remembered the name. Tac Fuhn—the mercenary from the war. Seventy-two was the year my father had served. I said, "It's the name of that Cambodian man in Vietnam."

He nodded. "I use that password on everything except my bank accounts. They require that I change the password yearly, so it's TacFuhn87. Start a new page. Write *Financial*."

"Okay."

"My investments are handled by Susan Balogh. Her number is 592-9145." He repeated the number slowly. "Write this down, it's very important. I have copies of everything inside the fire safe in my den. It's in the bottom drawer of my gray file cabinet. It requires a key and a combination. The key is in the top drawer of my desk next to the credit card. You'll recognize the key. It's one of those stubby ones with a black plastic bow."

"A black what?"

"Bow. It's the part of the key left outside the lock."

That was the kind of detail only my father would know.

"The key next to it, the funny-looking one, is for my safe deposit box at Chase. I've put you down as an owner, so you'll have access. The combination to the safe is 4-16-63. The instructions are on a sheet next to the key. I think you turn clockwise until you pass the first number three times, then counterclockwise . . . You don't need to write this down, it's on the instructions. You've opened a safe before, haven't you?"

"Of course."

"There's nothing in there that Susan can't help you with. I have an IRA, a Keogh, three mutual funds, and two insurance policies. You are the sole beneficiary. After I die, you can do what you like with the funds, but I don't recommend that you cash out in one lump sum. You'll get slaughtered by taxes, and the temptation to blow it all might be too great.

"I don't expect you to remember that; just call Susan.

I've already talked her through all of this. She'll help you set up an annuity with a monthly dividend. If you don't go crazy and loot the principal, there's enough in there to take care of you for the rest of your life."

I was feeling more and more uncomfortable with the conversation. But my father had always been direct. "Why do you have two insurance policies?"

"It's complicated. Each one has a different investment vehicle, but since you'll be awarded the death benefit, it doesn't matter." He closed his eyes for a moment, then said, "Write down *Home*." Again, I did as he said. "The house is paid for, so you can live there. Or, if you decide to move back to Seattle, you can sell it. Whichever suits you. You know I'm not sentimental. It's your house; do with it what you will.

"If you decide to sell, I recommend that you work with—write this down—Michelle Tripp. She goes by Shelly. I've known her for almost twenty years. She's one of my clients and is one of the top real estate agents in Pasadena. She helped me find my office and negotiate the rate. She'll take good care of you.

"I know this is a little overwhelming, but most everything I've just told you you'll find typed up inside the top drawer of my desk next to the keys. It's in a yellow file folder. You can't miss it. It has your name on it."

I wrote this down on my pad. When I looked back up my father was staring at me. "Any questions?"

"No, sir."

"Then you're not thinking about it hard enough."

"I'm sure I'll have questions later."

His gaze faltered, and he rubbed his chin. Then he said, "It's good that you're prepared. Who knows if I'll ever leave this place?"

I felt anger rise up in my chest. "Why all this talk about death? You're still young."

"Everyone dies."

"Not at your age," I said. We both knew it was foolish to say. My mother had been much younger when she died.

"You're right," he said. He looked down for a moment as if he were thinking, then he said, "You know that dream I told you about? The one about your mother and McKale?"

"Yes."

"You asked what I left out . . ." He paused. "Mom said I wasn't expected yet . . . but that I'd be with her very soon."

Neither of us spoke for a moment. Then I said, "It was only a dream."

He looked at me sympathetically and said, "You're right. It was only a dream." The room fell into silence again. After a moment he said, "Let me look through your notes."

I handed him the notepad. He looked through it, then gave it back to me. "You got everything." He leaned back and closed his eyes. "I think I'll take a nap. You can go if you like."

I sat there fighting my growing emotion. Finally I said, "Okay. Have a good rest."

"Al."

"Yes?"

"I love you, Son."

The words caught me off guard. "I love you too," I said.

◦⟩⟨◦

I drove back to the house, my mind reeling from our conversation. I realized that I had preferred living in denial, something my father, always the pragmatist, did not. *It didn't mean he was going to die*, I told myself. *He was just being prepared*. My excuse rang hollow.

My cell phone rang a little after ten. It was Nicole.

"Your father told me he'd had an uncomfortable discussion with you, but he wouldn't tell me what it was about."

"We went over his funeral plans."

She hesitated. "You know how he is. Planful."

My father loved to use that word. *Planful*.

"Is that even a real word?" I asked.

"Your dad might have invented it."

I breathed out slowly. "He told me that he loves me."

"He does love you."

"I know. But it's not like him to say it." I hesitated a moment. "He's planning on dying."

"You can't be sure of that."

"Yes, I can. It's like you said. He's planful."

There was a long pause, then she said, "What can I do for you?"

"Just being here is enough."

"Call if you need anything. I mean it. Call anytime."

My reply caught in my throat. "Thank you. Good night."

"Good night, Alan," she said.

I slowly hung up the phone. Part of me wanted to be back out on the road, where I could hide from this. I tried to watch television, but nothing kept my interest. I went to bed, but I couldn't sleep. Finally, at two in the morning, I surrendered to my insomnia. I turned the light on and opened the family history. It was time to finish reading what my father had written.

VII

A New World

Kate's death was the most difficult thing I have ever experienced. I felt as if I had been ripped in two. As hard as it was for me, I think it was even worse for Alan. His entire world seemed shattered. He was changed. Once I had to get angry with him to get him to eat because he'd lost so much weight. A couple times I found him crying, once in his closet.

Pretending to live as we had before was like living a lie. It wasn't long before I came to the conclusion that we needed to make a new life or be consumed by the old one.

A few weeks before I had come to this conclusion, a friend of mine from college had contacted me to tell me he was taking over his father's auto dealership in Pasadena. He needed someone to handle his accounting. He even offered space in his office where I could start my own CPA firm. At the time I told him I would think it over. Now the idea appealed to me.

One of Kate's neighborhood friends took Alan in while I flew to California. I found us a little home on Altura Street in Arcadia, just east of Pasadena. I met one of the neighbors, a recently divorced man with a girl who was Alan's age. He told me that the area was a good place to raise a family. I put an offer down on the home, then came back and told Alan that we were going to move. He didn't seem any more upset than he already was, which I took as a good sign.

We moved just five weeks later. While uprooting our lives was difficult at first, the change turned out to be good for Alan, as it kept him occupied. Not long after our move he became friends with McKale Richardson, the girl next door, and from then on he spent most of his time with her. I think she filled a hole his mother left.

VIII

And So It Goes

Five years after Kate's passing I met a woman named Gretchen O'Connor. She was a saleswoman at the car dealership. I suppose she reminded me of Kate in both looks and personality. Like me, she had lost her spouse to cancer. She had four children, the youngest just eighteen months old. I considered marrying her; we even talked about it, but she was so focused on the circumstances of her own children and their pain that I worried about how much attention and love she could provide Alan. As much as I desired companionship, I decided that she wouldn't be good for him and I told her that it would be best if we didn't see each other anymore. Saying goodbye wasn't easy for either of us, but I have never regretted the decision. My son needed me.

As I read this I felt ashamed. More than once I had criticized him for not finding love again. I had never known, never even really considered, just how much my father had sacrificed for me. He had given up his job and home in Denver, then the chance to marry again. How could I have been so unaware? How could I have been so ungrateful?

Life went on. In January 2001 Alan informed me that he was going to ask McKale to marry him. I thought that they were still a little young to get married, but he was smart and I'm not one to intervene in his choices. She accepted his proposal, and they were married on October 28, 2001.

Alan was accepted to the Art Center College of Design, and he and McKale moved to an apartment in West Pasadena, near the school. The house was quiet without my son. I was grateful to see them most Sundays, when we gathered for dinner.

Just three weeks after Alan graduated he was offered a job with Conan Cross, a prestigious advertising firm in Seattle. I was pleased that he got the position but upset that he would be living so far away. He did well at the agency and won a wall-full of awards.

Three years later Alan struck out on his own, starting a firm called Madgic. Again, it seemed as if my son could do no wrong. The firm grew by leaps and bounds, and Alan continued to win award after award. He and McKale purchased a large, beautiful home in Bridle Trails, an upscale suburb near Bellevue. Then, on September 8, 2011, McKale was thrown by a horse and broke her back, paralyzing her from the waist down. A month later she died of an infection. During this time Alan's business partner, whose name does not merit mention here, stole all of his clients, leaving my son bankrupt.

Alan had lost everything a man holds dear: his sweetheart, his home, and his business. The loss of any one of those things has brought lesser men to their destruction, but my son has persevered.

I learned in the jungles of Vietnam that when faced with overwhelming loss and stress, a man must choose to live and find his own way through his broken heart. Alan chose to endure. He decided to walk away from Seattle, Washington, to as far as he could go in the continental

United States—Key West, Florida—the very place our family story began.

As of this writing, Alan has nearly completed his journey. I have no doubt that he will. I don't know if it was a coincidence that led him to Key West or if maybe he was guided by some ethereal force, but either way, Alan has shown himself to be a man of courage and substance. He is a good man with a good heart—his mother's heart. It is hard for me to fully express my feelings to him, but I love him more than I could ever say. I am honored to be his father.

My father's writing ended there. I turned the page. There was a note in an unsealed envelope taped to the inside back of the binder. I extracted the paper from the envelope. The note was handwritten in my father's disciplined script.

My dear son,

This brings our family history to the present. The rest of the story is yours to complete. You are the last leaf on this branch of the Christoffersen family tree. Whether your leaf turns into another branch, or even another tree, is up to you and God. Should you choose to continue our family name, then this book will contain your story and your children's and grandchildren's stories as well. Your experiences on your walk will be a great addition to our family history and will inspire all who read it.

I have compiled this history so that someday, after I'm gone, you will know who you are and where you belong. Always remember that you are not alone. I may not have always said it, but I always tried to show you that I love you. I am proud to be your father. Always remember this, my son, and Godspeed, until you have finished your walk to Key West and your even greater journey after.

I finally understood. My father hadn't written our family history for himself. He'd written it for me. Only for me. He knew that someday he'd be gone and I would be completely alone. He was giving me a harbor from the squalls of time; he was giving me a place to belong.

CHAPTER

Sixteen

It is the heroic spirits in flawed men of flesh—not the whitewashed, heroic-sized renditions society fabricates—that deserve our adulation.

Alan Christoffersen's diary

I brought the book with me to the hospital the next morning. There was so much I wanted and needed to say to my father. Most of all, I wanted to thank him for all he had done for me. For all the sacrifices he had made for me.

When I arrived he was still asleep. I sat down next to his bed and looked at him, my heart full of emotion. Now I knew the Great and Powerful Oz was not an illusion. The man behind the curtain was far greater than the contrived illusion of my flawed childhood perspective. What would I say to him? I sat there for nearly two hours listening to his heavy breathing, worrying about what to say. I never got the chance.

Suddenly my father's breathing stopped, then he groaned. His eyes opened wide and he looked over at me. "Al . . ."

"Dad?"

He clutched his chest and grimaced. Perspiration beaded on the side of his face. An alarm went off.

"Dad, what's wrong?"

"Alan," he said. Another alarm went off.

I jumped up. "I'll get help." I ran out of the room. A nurse was already hurrying toward us. "I think my father's having another heart attack," I said.

The nurse ran into the room. She looked at my father, then shouted out the doorway to the woman sitting at the nurses' station. "I need some help in here. Get me an EKG and page the doctor."

I put my hand on my father's shoulder. He was clutching his chest and breathing heavily. Suddenly he went limp. "Dad, stay with me."

The nurse tilted my father's head back, then put two fingers to his wrist. "Mr. Christoffersen? He isn't breathing. Code blue!" She pushed a button on the wall next to the bed, then turned to me. "Stand back, please." She lowered the side bar of the hospital bed and began performing chest compressions.

I heard a voice over the intercom. "Code blue, second floor, room B237."

Two more women ran into the room, one pushing a cart packed with medical equipment. They rolled my father onto his side and placed a board under him. The nurse continued doing chest compressions.

The room exploded with action as more people began rushing in. One nurse put a mask over my father's nose and mouth while another placed pads on his chest.

I stepped back toward the corner of the room, my eyes riveted on my father. "What's going on?" I asked.

"He's gone into cardiac arrest," the first nurse said.

Just then Dr. Witt hurried in. He looked at the monitor on the cart and began directing the rest of the team. "Give him one milligram of epinephrine," he said.

A nurse inserted a syringe into my father's IV. "One milligram of epinephrine in."

"Pause the compressions," Dr. Witt said. He studied the screen for a moment. "Start again. We have a shockable rhythm. Let's prime one more minute and then we'll start. Two hundred joules." The defibrillator made a high-pitched noise as it charged up.

"Clear."

My father's body heaved.

"Two hundred joules delivered," said the nurse.

"Continue CPR for two minutes, then check for a pulse," Dr. Witt said.

"No pulse," the nurse said.

"Again," Dr. Witt said.

Again my father's body jumped.

An alarm went off. They repeated the cycle many more times, but my father showed no response.

After what felt like hours, the doctor turned to me. "I'm sorry." He said to the nurse, "Stop the compressions. I'm calling it." He looked at the clock. "Time of death is eight fifty-three."

One of the nurses walked to the machine and pushed some buttons. The room suddenly became quiet. Dr. Witt turned back to me. "Alan, I'm sorry. We did everything we could, but your father is dead."

Even though I had witnessed the entire scene, the pronouncement still, somehow, came as a shock. I walked to the side of the bed, and the nurses stepped aside, allowing me to take my father's hand and feel the last of his warmth. I leaned over him and kissed his forehead. Already the heat was leaving his body. The difference just a few seconds of life make—just a few breaths make. I felt cheated. I still had things I wanted to tell him. There was gratitude left unexpressed. I knelt down next to his bed and wept.

CHAPTER

Seventeen

The last line to my past has snapped. My father is gone.

Alan Christoffersen's diary

Everyone just stood around the bed for a moment; then Dr. Witt touched my arm, said he was sorry, turned, and left. The nurses followed him out.

I don't know how long they left me alone, but it seemed a while. Then one of the nurses walked back into the room. She said to me gently, "If it's okay with you, I'm going to pull the sheet up."

I nodded. I watched as she draped the sheet over his head. I stood there, still. More time passed. A petite, thirtysomething woman walked into the room. She had long, nut-brown hair pulled back over her elvish ears. She wasn't dressed as a nurse, and even though I had never seen her before, I knew who she was. Or at least why she was there. A social worker had come to me after McKale's death.

"Alan?" she said softly.

"Yes."

"I'm Gina. I'm a social worker for the hospital. I'm so sorry for your loss."

I didn't reply.

"If you would like to talk, I'd be happy to."

"I'll be okay," I said.

"Do you have any questions about what will happen now?"

I shook my head. "No. I just went through this with

my wife . . ." My eyes filled with tears, and I was unable to speak. The woman looked at me sympathetically, then reached out and touched my arm. "I'm so sorry."

After a moment I said, "I can't think. What do I need to do?"

"Your father's body will be kept in the hospital mortuary until you arrange for a funeral director to collect it. Have you made any contacts, or would you like some help?" I swallowed, trying to compose myself. "Take your time," she said.

I breathed out slowly. "He made arrangements . . . Beard Mortuary."

"I'm familiar with them," she said. "Would you like me to contact them for you?"

I nodded. "Thank you."

"In just a moment we will bring you a medical certificate that shows the cause of death. You'll need to register the death and a few other minor details. There's a little checklist to help. Do you know if he wanted his body cremated?"

"He's going to be buried in Colorado. Next to my mother."

She nodded. "Very well. Let me go see if I can expedite the certificate." She left the room.

A minute after she left I took out my phone and called Nicole.

"Hi," she said. "I'm on my way over right now."

I didn't respond. Emotion had frozen me.

"Alan?"

"He's had another heart attack," I said. "He's gone."

There was a long pause. Then I heard her crying. In a muffled voice she said, "I'll be right there."

The social worker returned carrying an envelope. "Here you are. I put the checklist inside. You'll need to sign the certificate, and we'll need to gather your father's possessions. The nurses will do that; I'll remind them."

"Thank you."

"I'm happy to help." She took out a business card. "Grief can be an unpredictable thing. If you change your mind and would like to talk, please give me a call."

❧

Nicole arrived a few minutes later. Her cheeks were tearstained and her eyes were red and puffy. She was out of breath. At first she looked only at me, afraid to look at my father. Then she turned toward his shrouded body. She gasped lightly. Then she softly said, "Oh, Bob." Tears fell freely down her cheeks.

She walked to the side of the bed and slowly peeled back the sheet. When she saw his face she groaned out, "No." She pulled the sheet back up, then turned back and fell into me. I wrapped my arms around her. She laid her head against my shoulder and began to sob with such emotion that I had difficulty holding her. "I'm so sorry," she said.

A few moments later a nurse walked in carrying a canvas bag. She waited until I looked at her. "I'm sorry to disturb you. These are your father's belongings. Would you mind signing that you received them?"

Without a word I signed the form.

"And the certificate," she said.

I took the form out of the envelope, signed it as well, and handed it back to the nurse.

"Thank you."

Nicole broke down crying again. I put our family history inside the bag. I don't know how long we were there.

A half hour, maybe more, but finally I couldn't stand being there any longer. "I need to go."

We both walked over to the bed. I touched my father once more. "Goodbye, Dad," I said. Then I walked out of the room.

Nicole came out a moment later. As I held her, Dr. Witt walked up to us.

"I'm sorry," he said, looking at Nicole. "There was nothing more I could do."

His tone wasn't that of a doctor, and I realized that there was something to what my father had said about them.

She looked into his eyes. "Thank you, Mark."

"May I check on you later?"

She nodded. "I'd like that."

He glanced over at me with an anxious expression, then turned and walked away. I looked at Nicole. I sensed that she wanted to say something about them, but it wasn't the time.

We took the elevator to the main floor and walked out to the parking lot. I stopped on the sidewalk and looked into Nicole's eyes. "Stay with me."

Her brow fell. "Alan . . ."

"I don't want to be alone," I said. "Would you come over? Please?"

She hesitated a moment, then said, "I need to get my things from the hotel."

I walked her to her car, where she broke down crying again. "I'll see you in a minute," she said. She wiped her eyes and climbed in.

I walked back to my father's car and drove to his house.

CHAPTER

Eighteen

While flailing about in an ocean of grief we must be mindful not to drown those trying to rescue us.

Alan Christoffersen's diary

There were more of the women's offerings on the porch when I got home. I didn't bother to pick them up or even look at them; I just pushed them out of the way with my foot. I went to my room and lay down on the bed to wait for Nicole. I heard her car pull into the driveway about twenty minutes later.

I opened the front door and met her on the porch. We embraced. After a moment she said, "Come here." She took my hand and led me inside to the dimly lit living room.

Heavy with grief, we sat next to each other on one end of the couch. Then she lay back and pulled me into her. I laid my head against her breast while she softly rubbed the back of my neck.

"I feel like everything's finally gone," I said. "There's nothing left to lose."

"You have a lot to lose," she said. I looked up at her. Her deep blue eyes locked on to mine. For a moment we just looked at each other. The power and complexity of our emotions rose around us like a vapor. Then the vacuum of our loss and want collapsed the void between us, drawing us to each other. We kissed. I pulled her into me, and our kissing grew more and more passionate. Suddenly she pulled away.

"Wait," she said breathlessly.

I looked at her. She had a blank, dazed expression.

"What's wrong?" I asked.

"It's not right," she said. "It doesn't feel right." She looked into my eyes. "I'm so sorry. It feels like—" she stopped. "You're going to think this is so weird after the way I've been chasing you . . ."

"What?"

Her face strained with pain. "Please don't take this wrong; you know how much I love you . . ."

I had no idea where she was going with this. "What, Nicole?"

"It feels like I'm kissing my brother."

CHAPTER

Nineteen

Déjà vu. Again. (I know that's redundant. I suppose that's my point.)

Alan Christoffersen's diary

The next morning I woke in the familiar haze of grief. It wasn't as heavy as it had been when I lost McKale, or even the same as when I'd lost my mother. It was different. When my mother died, it felt like my world had ended. When McKale died, my future had vanished. When my father died, I felt like I'd lost my past.

Nicole had slept upstairs in my old bedroom, and now I could hear her outside the room where I'd slept. I didn't know what time it was, but my room was bright with a late sun. I pulled on the shirt and pair of pants I'd worn the day before and walked out to the kitchen. It smelled of bacon and pancakes.

"Hi," Nicole said sweetly.

I raked my hair back with my hand. "What time is it?"

"It's almost eleven," she said. She took the frying pan off the flame and came over and hugged me. "I'm glad you got some sleep. The next morning is always the hardest." She held me for a moment, then asked, "Are you hungry?"

"Yes."

"I made blueberry pancakes and bacon."

"Where did you get the food?"

"I had to go shopping. All your dad had was Wheaties and TV dinners." She walked back to the stove. "Sit. I'm just about done."

I sat down at the table. Nicole brought over a stack of pancakes with a glass of orange juice, then another plate with bacon. "Go ahead and start," she said. "I just need to finish this pancake."

I poured syrup over the stack. "How'd you sleep?" I asked.

"Not very well," she said. "I got up early." She brought her plate to the table and sat down across from me. "As you can see."

"Thank you," I said.

"It's okay, I like cooking. It's peaceful."

"I meant for not leaving me," I said.

She smiled sadly. "You're my best friend. You always will be."

"Like a brother, huh?"

"I'm sorry. I don't know what to say." She looked at me sheepishly. "You don't feel bad, do you? I mean, you're the one who rejected me first."

"It's just a bruised ego," I said.

"I'm sorry."

"At least I don't have to worry about you disappearing on me again."

"No, you don't," she said. She leaned forward and kissed me on the cheek, then sat back down. "So what are you doing today?"

"Details," I said. "My father left me a checklist. This morning I need to call the mortuary and set a date for the viewing."

"They beat you to it," she said. "They called an hour ago. I wrote the number down next to the phone. What day is the viewing?"

"I need to decide. I don't even know what day it is today."

"It's Tuesday."

"Maybe we should have it this Friday."

"Friday would be good," she said. "That should give the mortuary enough time." She looked at me for a moment, then said, "Then what?"

"After I take care of everything here, I'll go back out."

She looked a little surprised. "You're going to finish your walk?"

I nodded. "It's odd, but there's a part of me that feels like I need to finish the walk as much for my father as for myself." I took a bite of the pancake, then asked, "What about you? What's next?"

"I was planning on staying until the viewing. Then I need to get back to Spokane to check on things. I talked to Kailamai last night, and she said one of the tenants was complaining about her plumbing. Sometimes I forget I'm a landlord." She sighed. "What do you need from me?"

"Just you," I said.

"Do you mind if I read your family history?"

"No. I think that would please my father."

Nicole was quiet a moment, then she said, "You need to call Falene." When I didn't reply, she said, "You need to call her today. She needs to know about your father. You need to share this with her."

"I know," I said.

Neither of us spoke for a moment. Then she said, "I think I know why you haven't called her."

"Why?"

"It's because deep inside you're afraid that she might have moved on. Sometimes it's easier to live with the uncertainty than to confront the truth."

I thought over her theory, then replied, "Maybe you're right."

"Call her," she said again. "Today. She deserves to know. So do you."

"All right," I said. "I'll call her."

CHAPTER

Twenty

I have found Falene only to discover that I
have less of an idea of where she is now than
I had before.

Alan Christoffersen's diary

After breakfast I returned the call to Beard Mortuary. As my father had told me in the hospital, he'd taken care of every possible detail—everything except the date of his viewing and the writing of his obituary. I scheduled a viewing at the Beard Mortuary Chapel for Friday evening. Then, with Nicole's help, I wrote my father's obituary.

Robert Alan Christoffersen
1953–2012

Robert "Bob" Alan Christoffersen, husband, father, and friend, unexpectedly passed away of heart failure on November 2, 2012, at the age of 59. Bob was born in Denver, Colorado. He was drafted into the Vietnam War, where he saw combat and was a highly decorated lieutenant of the First Air Cavalry. He returned from the war and enrolled at the University of Colorado in Boulder, where he graduated in accounting. He married his high school sweetheart, Kate Mitchell, in 1974. In 1979 Kate gave birth to their son, Alan. Eight years later his sweetheart passed away from cancer, and he never remarried. Bob was a skilled CPA and worked eleven years for Peat Marwick of Denver before moving to Pasadena, where he opened his own firm. Bob was a good man with impeccable integrity and will be missed by all who knew him. He is survived only by his son, Alan Christoffersen. A viewing will be held at the Beard Mortuary Chapel at 396 Colorado Blvd. on Friday night from six to nine p.m. He has requested that in lieu of flowers, donations be sent to the American Red Cross, Los Angeles Region, at www.redcross.org or the American Cancer Society at https://donate.cancer.org.

Nicole read it over. "Do you need to put in the Web addresses?"

"It was my father's idea," I said.

"Then it's perfect," Nicole said.

I took a deep breath. "It seems so inadequate."

"I know," Nicole replied. "How do you condense someone's life into a couple of paragraphs?"

❧

While Nicole went shopping for a dress for the service, I sat down to read over my father's checklist.

I've heard horror stories of people settling their parents' estates, but they didn't have my father watching over them. He knew I wasn't good with money, so he had pretty much taken care of everything.

When I first started making a decent salary in Seattle, I went to him for financial advice. He was explaining the pros and cons of different types of IRAs and investment funds when finally I stopped him and said, "Hold on, I have no idea what you're talking about. Explain this to me like I'm ten years old." A minute later I stopped him again. "Explain it like I'm five years old," I said, which is exactly what he did. And he was still doing it. Each document was accompanied by a page with step-by-step instructions, contacts, and phone numbers.

Financially, my father had left me more than I even knew he had. I didn't know that he was a millionaire, but that shouldn't have surprised me. He once told me that most millionaires don't live like millionaires—that it is usually the faux millionaires who go for the show: driving expensive, depreciating cars and living in over-sized homes mortgaged to their rooftops. (At the time I suspected he was trying to make a point, as McKale and I fit his description.) My father was industrious, a skilled money manager, and religiously frugal—a combination that pretty much guaranteed financial success.

Nicole was gone less than two hours. After she returned we went over my father's funeral list. There was a spread-sheet listing the names of his friends and clients with their contact information. At the bottom of the list he had added, *And anyone else you would like to invite.*

Nicole looked up at me. "Did you call Falene?"

"Not yet."

"You should do it now."

"I'll get to it."

"Now," she said.

"Why are you suddenly so interested in me calling her?"

"Maybe because I suffered enough over not having you and I want at least to know it wasn't in vain."

"All right," I said. "I'll call."

Walking on Water

I went to my room and found the note Falene had written me when she left St. Louis.

My dear Alan,

Sometimes a girl can be pretty deaf to the things she doesn't want to hear. Or maybe it's just easy to ignore the answers that are shouted but never spoken. I should have heard your answer in your silence. I've asked you twice if I could be there when you arrived in Key West and you never answered me. I should have known that was my answer. If you had wanted me there, you would have answered with a loud "yes." Forgive me for being so obtuse (I learned that word from you). But there's a good reason I ignored the obvious. The truth was too painful. You see, I love you. I'm sorry that you had to learn it here, so far from me. I looked forward to the day when I could say it to your face. But I now know that day will never come.

I love you. I know this. I really, truly, deeply love you. I first realized that I had fallen in love with you about two months after I started working at the agency.

Of course, I wasn't alone. I think all the women at your agency had a crush on you. Why wouldn't they? You were handsome and funny and smart, but most of all, you had a good heart. Truthfully, you seemed too good to be true. You were also loyal to your wife, which made you even more desirable.

Up until I met you, I thought all men were users and abusers. Then you had to come along and ruin my perfect misandry. You are everything a man should be. Strong but gentle, smart but kind, serious but fun with a great sense of humor. In my heart I fantasized about a world where you and I could be together. How happy I would be to call you mine!!

I know this will sound silly and juvenile, like a schoolgirl crush, but I realized that your name is in my name. You are the AL in FALENE. (As you can see, I've spent way too much time fantasizing about you!) But that's all it was. Fantasy.

When McKale died I was filled with horrible sadness and concern for you. I was afraid that you might hurt yourself. Seeing the pain you felt made my love and respect for you grow even more. Please forgive me, but the afternoon of the funeral, when I brought you home, I believed, or hoped, for the first time, that someday you might be mine. I didn't feel worthy of you, but I thought that you, being who you are, might accept me.

When you told me you were going to walk away from Seattle, I was heartbroken. I was so glad that you asked me to help you, giving me a way to stay in your life. Then, when you disappeared in Spokane I was terrified. I didn't sleep for days. I spent nearly a hundred hours hunting you down. I'm not telling you this so you'll thank me, I just want you to finally know the truth about the depth of my feelings.

But, like I said, a girl can be pretty deaf sometimes. I wanted to hear you say that you loved me and cared about me as more than just a friend. It was a stupid dream. Yesterday, when I saw how close you are to beautiful Nicole, my heart was breaking. I realized that I had already lost my one chance of being yours. And there I was with nothing to offer. Not even my apartment in Seattle to go to anymore.

I didn't tell you, but I took the job in New York. I needed to get out of Seattle. I failed to save my brother. I failed to save your agency. I failed to make you love me. I've failed at everything I've hoped for.

I'm sorry I didn't finish the task you gave me. I gave all your banking information to your father. He'll do a better job than I could anyway. I'm so sorry to not be at your side in your time of need, but it is now obvious to me that you don't need me. I'm just noise in the concert of your life. And this time I need to be selfish. I have to be. The risk to my heart is too great. They say that the depth of love is revealed in its departure. How true that is. I'm afraid that I'm just learning how deep my love is for you, and it's more than I can stand. I love you too much to just be a bystander in your life.

Well, I guess I've finally burned the bridge. I couldn't help myself. Please forgive me for being so needy. Please think of me fondly and now and then remember your starry-eyed assistant who loves you more than anything or anyone else in this world.

I know you will reach Key West. I know you'll make it and that you'll be okay. That's all I need. It's not all I want, but it's all I need—to know that you are okay and happy. Damn, I really love you.

Be safe, my dear friend. With all my love,

Falene

I took out my phone and listened to Carroll's message for Falene's phone number. I took a deep breath, then dialed.

Someone answered on the first ring. *"Pronto."* There was loud music in the background, and I couldn't tell if it was Falene's voice.

"Hello? Falene?"

"Hold on a minute, please. I need to step outside."

A moment later the voice said, "Hi, sorry about that. Who is this?"

I recognized her voice. "Falene, it's me." When she didn't respond I added, "Alan."

There was an even longer pause. "Alan. How did you find me?"

"It wasn't easy."

"Are you in Key West?"

"No. I'm in Pasadena."

"You're still sick?"

"No. My father had a heart attack."

Her voice softened. "Oh, Alan. Is he okay?"

"He passed away yesterday."

"I'm so sorry."

For a moment neither of us spoke. I finally broke the silence. "How are you doing? How's New York?"

"It's not Seattle," she said. "But it's good."

"Are you modeling?"

"Yes. Full-time."

"How's it going?"

"It's going well. I did a shoot for *Maxim* last week. It's not a cover, but it's good just to make the magazine, you know. And I have a contract with a new energy drink company. We start shooting next week."

In spite of my pain I felt happy for her. "Congratulations."

"Thank you."

After a moment I said, "I miss you."

She hesitated, then said softly, "I miss you too."

"You left without saying goodbye."

"I just thought it would be best . . . under the circumstances."

"What circumstances? That I had a tumor?"

"No," she said, angrily. "Have I ever left you in need?"

"Not until now."

"That's not fair," she said.

"I'm sorry; you're right." More silence. I felt stupid. I *was* stupid. *Why would I attack her when I was trying to get her back?* I waited for her to say something, but after a moment it didn't seem that she would.

"I saw your brother."

"You saw Deron? Where?"

"In Seattle. He's in jail." I regretted the words as they came out of my mouth. *More pain.* I was surprised that she didn't just hang up on me. "I'm sorry."

"I haven't heard from him since May, when he started using again," Falene said. "How did you find him?"

"I was looking for him."

"Why would you do that?"

"I was hoping he could tell me how to find you. You did a good job of disappearing."

"You went to all that work to find me?"

"Of course I did."

She was quiet a moment, then asked, "When is your father's funeral?"

"It's just a viewing. It's this Friday."

"In Pasadena?"

"Yes."

"Would you mind if I came out?"

"I was hoping you would."

"We can talk then," she said. "There are things to be said." Her voice was laced with sadness.

I breathed out slowly, wondering what she meant. "Okay," I said. "We'll talk then."

"I'd like to contact my brother. Can you tell me where he is?"

"He was in the King County jail in Seattle."

"Thank you. And thank you for looking for me."

"Like you did when I disappeared in Spokane."

She didn't reply.

"Call me when you're in town," I said.

"I will. Bye."

"Goodbye," I said.

I hung up the phone. The call hadn't gone the way I'd hoped it would. Actually, I'm not sure what I'd hoped for—except that she would sound more excited to hear from me. Or that she would tell me she still loved me. Instead, it sounded as if something had changed in the time we'd been apart.

Nicole was in the living room reading the family history when I walked in. She set the binder down. "Did you call?"

"Yes."

"How did it go?"

"I don't know."

"You don't know?"

I shook my head. "No. But she's coming out for the viewing."

CHAPTER

Twenty-One

Kailamai is back. Fortunately she brought her
jokes with her.

Alan Christoffersen's diary

The next two days were busy, which was a blessing, as it kept my mind from all the things I would rather not think about, including my conversation with Falene. Something had clearly changed. Still, she was coming out. That had to be significant.

I systematically worked down my father's list. I decided that until I knew what I was going to do after I finished my walk I would just keep the house. Maybe I would live in Pasadena for a while. Maybe forever. At this point anything was possible.

Kailamai flew in from Spokane on Thursday night around six.

Kailamai was the young woman I had rescued from a group of men just outside of Coeur d'Alene, Idaho. She had run away from her foster care family just before her eighteenth birthday. I had connected her with Nicole, and the two of them now lived together.

We went directly from LAX to dinner, a little sushi restaurant in Pasadena called Matsuri. It had been more than six months since I'd seen Kailamai, and she had changed quite a bit. Her appearance was different. She looked like a student. She wore a Gonzaga college sweat-shirt and purple-framed glasses. She had taken out her nose piercing and wore only one pair of earrings. But the more significant change was less tangible. She seemed . . .

domesticated. After we had ordered our meals Kailamai said, "I'm so sorry about your dad."

"Thank you. He was a good man."

"Nicole said that all the time. She's going to miss him."

"We all will," Nicole said.

"So how's school?" I asked.

"It's going really well," Kailamai said.

"Straight As," Nicole said.

"And I met someone."

Nicole's eyes widened.

"Someone?" I asked.

"His name is Matt. He's also prelaw. He's pretty special."

"This is news," Nicole said.

"Well, you've been gone like two weeks. Things happen fast with me."

"Apparently," Nicole replied.

"You'll meet him when we get back. If you ever come back."

"I'm coming back," Nicole said.

Kailamai turned to me. "How far have you gotten on your walk? The last I heard you were in Alabama."

"I made it to the northern border of Florida—a little town called Folkston."

"Are you still going to finish?"

"I'm planning to."

"And we're planning on being there when you arrive in Key West," she said. "So just make sure you don't do it around any of my finals."

Nicole rolled her eyes.

After we had started eating, Kailamai said, "So a woman is sitting in a bar when someone says, 'Hey, you're really hot.' She looks around but can't see anyone looking at her. Then she hears, 'Is that a new blouse? You're lookin' good, girl.' She suddenly realizes that it's the bowl of pretzels in front of her that's talking. She tries to ignore it and orders a Chardonnay. The pretzels say, 'Hmm, Chardonnay. You're one classy babe.' The woman says to the bartender, 'Hey, your pretzels keep saying nice things to me.' The bartender replies, 'They do that. They're complimentary.'"

"You live with this?" I asked Nicole.

"Daily," she said.

"She loves me," Kailamai said.

Nicole lifted a piece of sushi with her chopstick. "I do," she replied. "But I also love raw tuna."

I went to bed around ten while Kailamai and Nicole stayed in the kitchen and talked. As I plugged in my cell phone to recharge it, I received a text from Falene. All it said was that she would be in LA around noon. I texted back to see if she needed a ride or a place to stay, but she didn't respond.

CHAPTER

Twenty-Two

Today I said goodbye to two people I love.

Alan Christoffersen's diary

I woke the next morning to Nicole's and Kailamai's voices in the kitchen. I pulled on a robe and walked out. The kitchen was a mess.

"Morning, sleepyhead," Nicole said.

"What are you concocting in here?" I asked.

"Eggs Benedict," Nicole replied. "It will be a few more minutes."

I sat down at the table. Kailamai sat down next to me. "Do you want to hear a joke?"

I rubbed a hand across my face. "Sure."

"A new preacher was asked to speak at a country funeral. He had never been to the area where the funeral was and he got lost in the woods. After wandering around for nearly an hour he came upon some men gathered around an open grave. The preacher apologized for being late and started in. Feeling bad that the deceased man only had the diggers around his grave, the preacher tried to make up for it by giving the best eulogy he could. He preached with such passion that even the workers were shouting, 'Praise God' and 'Glory be!'

"After the eulogy one of the diggers said to the preacher, 'Preacher, that was inspirin'. I ain't never seen anything like that before, and I've been puttin' in septic tanks for twenty years!'"

"Kailamai," Nicole said indignantly. "Really?"

She flushed. "I asked if he wanted to hear it."

"About a funeral?" Nicole said.

"I'm sorry," Kailamai said.

"It's okay," I said. I whispered to her, "It was pretty funny."

Kailamai grinned furtively. "I thought so."

A few minutes later Nicole brought over our breakfasts.

"You really don't need to go to all this trouble," I said. "I'm used to eating light."

"Who said I'm doing it for you?" she said, grinning.

∽

After Kailamai went upstairs to get ready, Nicole said, "I'm sorry about that joke. Kailamai doesn't know how to deal with death."

"That makes two of us," I said. "After all she's been through, it's amazing the changes she's made. You've done a remarkable job with her."

"Thank you," Nicole said. "Sometimes I feel like I'm her mother."

"You are," I said.

She smiled. A moment later she asked, "Have you heard from Falene?"

"Just a text. She said her flight will be in around noon."

"That's good." She breathed out. "Are you picking her up?"

"I offered, but she never responded."

"Give her some time," Nicole said. "Things will work out."

∽

The rest of the afternoon passed in a blur. Unlike Nicole, I hadn't really thought about what I would wear to the viewing, and I ended up running out at the last moment to buy some loafers, a dress shirt, and a two-piece suit. I got home just in time to shower and get dressed. I borrowed one of my father's ties.

Before leaving I went to my room and got the letter that Falene had written. I folded it in half and put it in my coat pocket.

Nicole suggested that we drive separately to the funeral home, so I would be free to stay out late with Falene. I wondered why I still hadn't heard from her.

The viewing was scheduled to start at six, and at the funeral director's request we arrived an hour early. I had taken just a few steps into the chapel when I froze. Seeing the casket at the front of the room brought forth a rush of such painful memories that I had to sit down. Nicole stood next to me, rubbing my back. It took me several minutes before I could look at my father's body.

He was dressed in his navy blue suit with a solid, light blue tie and a matching handkerchief. After I had walked away from the casket Nicole and Kailamai approached. Nicole said softly, "He looks good."

"For being dead," Kailamai replied.

"Stop it," Nicole said.

"I'm sorry," Kailamai said.

❧

The chapel wasn't large, but it was more than sufficient for the modest attendance we expected. In one corner of the room there was a Steinway grand piano. Near the entry-way there was a round burled walnut table with an easel holding a gold-framed picture of my father in his military dress uniform and a wedding picture of my parents. There was also a felt-lined case of his war medals, something my mother had put together for him before I was born. I hadn't provided the memorabilia, so I assumed my father had left it with them years before.

A few minutes before six o'clock a woman sat down at the piano and began playing "The Impossible Dream" from *Man of La Mancha*. If lives had theme songs, "The Impossible Dream" would have been my father's.

Guests began arriving a few minutes before the hour. There was a sizable crowd, much larger than I'd expected. It was a testament to the man my father was. I believe every client he'd ever had was there.

I stood next to the casket and thanked people for coming. Some of them were grieving heavily, and I heard story after story about how good my father had been to people. I felt sad that I hadn't known all this about him, but my father wasn't one to talk about the good that he'd done.

There were many women, some whose names I recognized from the packages that had been left on the doorstep over the last few weeks. An attractive, middle-aged woman with short, dark hair introduced herself as Gretchen O'Connor. I remembered the name from the family history. She was the woman my father almost married. I noticed that she wasn't wearing a wedding ring.

There were many of my father's buddies from Vietnam. They approached the casket as a group. They spoke of my father's courage and leadership. One told me that a common occurrence in Vietnam was fragging, where platoon leaders were so disliked by their soldiers that they were killed by grenades thrown by their own men. He said, "That never would have happened with your father. Every one of us would have taken a bullet for him." As he said this all the men nodded in agreement.

An hour into the viewing Nicole brought me a glass of water. "Are you doing okay?"

"Yes."

"Has she come?"

"Not yet," I said.

"She'll come," she said.

∾

It was a little past eight thirty when I saw Falene standing at the end of the line, near the chapel entrance. As always she looked strikingly gorgeous. Still, she looked different. Though she always dressed nicely, tonight her clothes looked *expensive*. It might sound strange to say it, but *she* looked expensive—her makeup and jewelry and shoes, even the way she carried herself. Her new world had changed her appearance. I wondered if the change was more than skin deep.

Our glances met, and I motioned for her to come up. Her beautiful brown eyes were filled with tears as she put her arms around me. "I'm so sorry, Alan. You don't deserve this."

I just held her. After we separated she said, "I'm sorry I'm so late."

"I was wondering if you were going to make it."

"Me too," she said. "The taxi driver took me to the wrong place. Twice. He barely spoke English."

"I'm glad you made it," I said. "You look beautiful."

She smiled sadly. "So do you." She glanced back at the line of mourners. "You have a lot of people here. We can talk after you're done." We embraced once more, then she walked to the back of the room.

It took another full hour to go through the rest of the line. One of the visitors was my father's friend Carroll, the private investigator who had found Falene for me. "I'm sorry for your loss," he said gruffly. "Your father was a fine man. A man's man. The world's a darker place without him."

"Thank you," I said.

"By the way, did you get my message about the woman you were looking for?"

I nodded. "Yes. Thank you. In fact, that's her right there."

He turned and looked at Falene, his gaze lingering on her longer than was appropriate. "Wow, she's a looker," he said, finally turning back. "No wonder you wanted to hunt her down. I'm glad that worked out."

I just nodded, bothered by his assessment but still in his debt for finding her. "Thanks for your help."

"Anything for your father," he said. "You make him proud."

❧

At one point I noticed Nicole talking to Falene. To my relief they both looked comfortable. When the line had finally dwindled, Nicole walked up to me. "Kailamai and I are going back to the house. Do you need anything?"

"I'm okay," I said. "Thank you for everything today."

She leaned forward and kissed my cheek. "Good luck." She walked off. Falene had been sitting quietly in a tucked leather chair across the room. She stood and walked to me. "May I see your father?"

"Of course."

She walked to the side of the casket. Her eyes filled with tears. I stepped up beside her. She said, "I know you two weren't always really close, but he loved you. When I was looking for you in Spokane . . . he was so upset." She turned and looked at me. "What I would have given to have had a father like that."

A moment later the funeral director walked up to us. "It's after nine thirty, so I've locked the front door," he said. "It was a beautiful evening—a real tribute to your father."

"It was nice," I said.

"I tell you, your father was a pleasure to work with. We don't need to talk about the details right now, but at your convenience, give us a call and we'll go over his burial plans in Colorado."

I nodded my assent.

"Oh, and on your way out remember to take your pictures and medal display. I'm sure you'll want those."

"Of course."

"I'm going to shut the casket now. Would you like another moment?"

"Please."

The director stepped aside. Again I approached the casket. I looked at him for a moment, then said, "Thank you for being my father. I hope you're with Mom." I closed my eyes as they filled with tears. Then I leaned forward, kissed his forehead, and turned to the director. "Okay." I stepped away from the casket, my eyes still fixed on my father's body.

The funeral director stepped forward. He reached inside the casket and unlatched the lid, then slowly shut it. Another pang of emotion filled my chest, and Falene put her hand on my lower back.

The director turned back to me. "I need to turn the lights out in about fifteen minutes. You can let yourself out the front door." He walked out of the room.

I took a deep breath, then turned to Falene. "We can talk in my car."

"Okay," she said softly. As long and as well as I had known her, at that moment I couldn't read her.

I collected the pictures from the display, and Falene carried the case of my father's medals.

"It's a beautiful night," I said.

"It's a lot warmer here than it is in New York. It was in the thirties at JFK. Maybe not even that."

"How was your flight?"

"Long," she said. "The guy sitting next to me had sneaked a fifth onto the plane. He was sloshed by the time we landed. He kept trying to touch me. The police had to carry him off."

"Lovely," I said.

"At least he didn't throw up on me," she said.

We put the pictures and medal case in the trunk. Then I opened the door for her and she climbed in. I got in the other side and started the car.

"Do you want to go somewhere?" I asked.

"Whatever you want," she replied.

❧

I drove to the arboretum. It was after hours and the park was closed, but after spending so much of my childhood there I knew how to sneak in. We walked in the dark along the back fence to a section of the grounds near a pond where McKale and I used to catch crayfish. There was a streetlamp about thirty yards from the bench, providing enough illumination for us to see. We sat down next to each other.

"This is where you got married, isn't it?" Falene said.

"Over there on the other side of the entry. It's a little better weather tonight." I looked into her eyes and could see the moon's reflection from the pond. "Thank you for coming," I said.

"I wanted to be here for you."

"You've always been there for me," I said.

"Except for when I wasn't," she replied. I guessed that she was referring to what I'd said to her on the phone, which made me regret saying it even more.

I said, "You asked how I found you. I hired a private investigator. It took him a while to track you down. I think he called every modeling agency in New York."

She looked at me quizzically. "Why would you go to so much trouble?"

"You don't know why?"

She lightly shook her head.

I reached in my pocket and pulled out the letter she had written me. "It's like you wrote: love doesn't know its depth until its absence. It wasn't until after you left that I knew how much you meant to me. And how much I wanted you in my life." I tried to read her face for a reaction, but she looked more upset by my confession than pleased. Finally I said, "I thought that's what you wanted."

She looked up at me. "You know I care about you, right?"

I hated the sound of that. She took a deep breath and slowly exhaled. "When I was a freshman in high school I wanted to make friends, so I tried out for cheerleading. You had to do this routine. I had never taken gymnastics or dance classes like the other girls, but I thought that maybe I could watch the others and learn fast.

"The tryouts were held after school. I sat there alone waiting my turn. Just before my routine a couple of the popular girls came up to me. I was nervous but kind of excited that they would talk to me. One of them said, 'What are you doing here?' I said, 'The same thing as you.' She rolled her eyes and said, 'I doubt that.' Then the other girl said, 'I guess they'll let anyone try out.'

"I was crushed. I still tried out, mostly just to show them that they couldn't intimidate me, but it was humiliating. And I failed miserably. They didn't even let me finish my routine. Those two girls became cheerleaders and I was the girl behind the bleachers with whatever boy wanted me. That experience taught me that the surest way to misery was to try to be something you're not."

"What does that have to do with us?"

"It has everything to do with us," she said. "Our worlds are completely different. I wanted to believe otherwise, but I was just lying to myself. Look at tonight. Your father loved you. I don't even know my father's name."

"And that was your fault?"

"It doesn't matter whose fault it is, it's just what it is. I'm from Stockton, you're from Pasadena. You graduated from one of the best graphic colleges in the country, I barely got out of high school."

"And you're smarter than most of my clients," I said. "You were a teenager and providing for your family, taking care of an alcoholic mother and keeping your brother off the streets. Half the graduates of Harvard couldn't have pulled off what you did."

"You don't get a degree for survival," she said.

"In the end, survival is the only degree that matters," I said. "It's the core human experience."

"Have you forgotten who I was before you found me? I worked in a strip club."

"I don't care about your past. Look at who you've become."

She shook her head. "Who I've become? I'm the same person I've always been. I used to think I had changed, but I haven't. Inside I'm still that same girl behind the bleachers. Even at the modeling agency. Why can't you see that?"

"Why can't you see how good you really are? When everything came crashing down in my life, you were the only one who was loyal. The *only* one. When my heart was broken and I was alone, you took me in. When I disappeared in Spokane, you looked for me until you found me. The only other person who has stood by me like that was McKale."

"I'm not McKale," she said angrily.

"I didn't say you were. I said you were loyal like her. And good like her."

"I'm not good."

"I *know* you're good, Falene. I've seen it. You don't think McKale had her faults?"

"McKale never danced nude for drunk old men."

"McKale was never homeless with a wayward brother."

She leaned closer and said softly, "Alan, you're not being honest. I am what I am."

"You're the one who's not being honest. I know who you are, even if you don't. I don't understand why you're doing this."

She turned away from me.

"You said you loved me," I said. "I love you too. That's the reality." I took her chin in my hand and lifted her head to look at me. Tears welled up in her eyes. "Falene, I'm willing to take a chance on us. Why won't you?"

She again turned away from me. Tears rolled down her cheeks. When she could speak she said softly, "Because I can't, Alan."

"Why not?" I said. "Give me one good reason."

She looked back, her eyes filled with tears. "Because I'm getting married."

I was stunned. When I could speak I said, "Married?"

She again turned away from me.

"To whom?"

It was a full minute before she spoke. "His name is Jason. He's one of the owners of the agency."

"How long have you known him?"

She didn't answer.

"Falene, how long have you known him?"

"It doesn't matter how long I've known him."

"Do you love him?"

Again she said nothing.

"I'll take that as an answer," I said.

"Love isn't everything," she blurted out.

I must have looked at her for a full minute before I said, "Then what is?"

She sat quietly for a moment, then stood up and walked back the way we had come in. She never answered my question.

❧

The drive to Falene's hotel was silent except for her occasional sniffling. I tried to think of something powerful to say, but words failed me. I parked in front of the hotel. We sat a moment in silence, then I said, "Whatever you've planned can be undone. It's not too late."

She looked at me with red, puffy eyes and said softly, "I love you, Alan. I always will. But it was too late before we even met." She leaned forward and kissed me on the cheek, then opened the door and walked into the hotel.

I just watched her disappear. My Dulcinea. I didn't think my heart could break more than it already had. But I was wrong.

CHAPTER

Twenty-Three

Two million steps forward, three million back.

Alan Christoffersen's diary

Nicole walked into my room around noon. I was sitting cross-legged on the floor going through my pack. Clothes and supplies were strewn all around me.

"Kailamai get off all right?" I asked.

Nicole nodded. "Yeah. Her flight was a little delayed, but it finally left." She sat down on my bed and sighed. "I'm sorry, Alan. I don't know what to say."

"Maybe some people just weren't meant to be happy," I said.

"You don't believe that."

"Maybe," I said.

She took a deep breath. "When are you leaving?"

"As soon as I finish my father's list. Maybe next Friday." I nodded as if I'd just made an agreement with myself. "Next Friday's good." I looked at her. "How about you?"

"Maybe I'll leave Friday too."

"You don't need to stay here for me."

"Yes I do," she said. The room fell into silence as I arranged my belongings. Nicole reached down and lifted the yellow envelope with my name written on it. "What's this?"

"My father asked me to take it with me to Key West."

"What's in it?"

"I don't know. He asked me not to open it until I get there."

She set the envelope back down. "How much longer will it take you to get to Key West?"

"It's a little more than five hundred miles. About a month."

"Then you'll get there just before Christmas."

"Probably. I'll call you when I reach Miami."

"And we'll be there when you cross the finish line. I promise."

We just looked at each other for a moment; then she held open her arms. "Come here."

I stood up and went and sat down on the bed next to her. She wrapped her arms around me. "I'm going to miss you. I love you, you know."

I laid my head on her shoulder. "It's a good thing. You're the only one left in my life."

CHAPTER

Twenty-Four

When you've got nowhere to go, walk.

Alan Christoffersen's diary

There's a saying among frequent fliers that the routes to heaven and hell pass through the Atlanta airport. I've mostly experienced the latter. The last time I passed through Atlanta I was worried about my father and anxious about Falene. Now, returning to Jacksonville through Atlanta, I was mourning both of them. My heart felt almost as heavy as it did leaving Seattle.

In Jacksonville I retrieved my pack from the carousel, then took a cab about forty miles northwest up Highway 1 to the town of Folkston, Georgia, where I had ended the last leg of my journey. Before leaving California I had again booked a room at the Inn at Folkston—the bed and breakfast I had stayed in before returning to California. The B&B had undergone a change of management since my last stay, so the new innkeepers, Pastor Ted and his wife, Alease, didn't know me. I doubted that the previous owners would have remembered me from my short stay, but B&B owners tend to make you feel like you're part of the family.

The room I had booked was called the Funnel Room— a peculiar name derived from the town's nickname, the Folkston Funnel. Because of its unique location, Folkston is on one of the busiest train routes in the world, and all the trains in Florida "funnel" through the small town. Train watchers (previous to my stay I hadn't known there was such a thing) come from all around the world to watch the trains pass through town—up to seventy a day.

Folkston also lays claim to being the Gateway to the Okefenokee—a title also claimed up north by Waycross, where I had toured the swamp.

I left my pack in my room, then returned to the front lobby. Pastor Ted was sitting in his office just right of the front door. He looked up from his paperwork as I walked by.

"May I help you with something?"

"I was just going to get some dinner," I said. "Do you have any recommendations?"

"If you like southern food, I'd recommend the Okefenokee Restaurant."

"Is it within walking distance?"

"Everything in Folkston is within walking distance," he said. "But the restaurant is only a few blocks from here. Just walk out the door, turn right, and go about five blocks. You'll see it on your right-hand side."

"I'll give it a try," I said. "So how's the inn business?"

"It's glorious," he said. "We're still getting our bearings, but Alease and I are both people people, so it's a treat getting to meet new people each day. It's like traveling without going anywhere."

"Are you from Folkston?"

"No, sir. I was born and raised in Jacksonville. As a matter of fact, I'm still the assistant pastor at the Jesus Christ Community Baptist Church in Jacksonville."

"How did you end up in Folkston?"

"The wife and I had decided to purchase a B&B once we retired. We'd been researching B&Bs for a couple of years, and one weekend we came up here to Folkston to get away for a few days. We asked the previous owners a lot of questions about the business. They asked why we were so curious. When we told them, they made us an offer we couldn't refuse. So I ended up taking an early retirement and we bought the place."

"And so far so good?"

He chuckled. "The wife hasn't left me yet, so yes. So far so good."

"Well, you hang on to her," I said. "I'll let you get back to work."

"Enjoy your dinner," he replied.

I followed his directions to the Okefenokee Restaurant. The walk was pleasant. The road was wide and lined with trees and interesting old homes. Many of the trees were draped in Spanish moss.

About halfway to the restaurant, the residential area turned into the business district, and I had to cross a wide swath of railroad tracks. There were people standing on both sides of the tracks waiting for trains.

The restaurant was just a couple blocks from the tracks. A young black woman with tightly braided hair and deep purple eye shadow greeted me at the door, then led me to the closest table, which was set with utensils rolled in paper napkins.

"We got our buffet," she said. "There's a menu too." She pointed to a folded sheet of paper. "You want something to drink?"

"Just water," I said.

"I'll get your water. If you decide to have the buffet, just help yourself. Most everyone just gets the buffet."

She walked away. I lifted the paper menu. I quickly deduced that you didn't have to order the buffet, but it was near sacrilege not to. The menu said:

If you don't want our buffet, this is what we can offer.

It offered a grilled cheese sandwich and hamburgers in various stages of dress. I got up and walked over to the buffet tables. Pastor Ted was right about the cuisine—it was as southern as cotton. There was okra, mustard greens, grits, fried catfish, fried shrimp, fatback, fried chicken, biscuits, and clam chowder. To the back of the room was a salad bar with sweet coleslaw and bread-and-butter pickles, which were delicious. I loaded up my plate, then went back to the table.

When my waitress returned with my water, I asked her what fatback was.

Her forehead furrowed. "You don't know what fatback is?"

"No, ma'am."

"It's fried bacon fat."

"Like chicharrón?" I asked.

She looked at me blankly. "I don't know what that is."

"Fried pork rinds?" I asked.

"Y'all just try it," she said. A moment later she returned with a bowl full of fried strips of fat. The first piece I tried was too chewy for my taste, and I ended up discreetly spitting it out and wrapping it in my napkin. *So much for fatback.*

The chicken and fish were good, as were the biscuits, but I wasn't used to ingesting so much fried food, and I left the restaurant with a stomachache.

As the sun fell, I walked back to the inn. The lights were on, and Ted and Alease were sitting on the porch next to two middle-aged women who were bent over a large cardboard box full of mail.

"Good evening," I said.

"Evening," they all replied.

"We'd shake your hand," the blond woman closest to

me said, "but we've been handling all this mail. I'm sure it's got nasty germs all over it."

"You get a lot of mail," I said. "You must be a celebrity."

The redheaded woman next to her laughed. "She's the queen of England," she drawled.

The blond woman shook her head. "It's my brother's mail. He's recently passed away, and we came down to settle his affairs. He had all this mail piled up."

I thought of my father and what I'd just been through working down his list. I thought of mentioning it but decided not to. "I'm sorry for your loss," I said.

"Thank you," she replied.

I sat down in a wicker chair between the pastor and his wife and the two women.

"How was dinner?" Ted asked.

"It was fine," I said. In a town as small as this it was likely that he knew the owner, and I didn't want to insult a friend of his.

As the sun set, the street fell into darkness. The moss on the trees looked as black and intricate as lace.

"It's beautiful here," I said.

"Yes it is," Ted said. "The leaves turn later in the South. One doesn't think of southern Georgia or Florida for changing leaves, but we've got red maple, sugarberry, persimmon, black cherry, maple, flowering dogwood, sassafras . . . Course, it's nothing like the Carolinas, but it's still beautiful."

"It's the snap of cold that turns the colors," Alease said. "So the farther south you go, the later the leaves turn. You'll see it. The turkey oaks turn a brilliant red in December."

"I love the Spanish moss," I said. "It's so uniquely southern. We don't have it on the West Coast."

"We've got plenty here," Ted said. "In the old days, they used it to stuff bed mattresses and furniture cushions. The problem is, it's full of chiggers."

Alease nodded. "You have to boil the moss before you use it. Otherwise, you'll get those chigger bites."

"Oh," groaned the redheaded woman. "Itches like the devil. A couple years ago I had them all over my legs. Took forever to get rid of them. They burrow under your skin."

"No they don't," the blond woman said. "They're just so small, you can't see them."

"Have you ever had chigger bites?" the redhead asked sharply.

"When I was a teenager," the blonde replied. She turned to me. "Have you ever had chigger bites?"

"Not that I know of," I said.

"You'd know if you had them," the redhead said.

"If you get them, don't scratch them," the blonde said. "That's when the torture really begins."

"It's best to put nail polish on them," the redhead said. "It reduces the itchiness."

"I've heard that," Alease said. "I'll have to try it."

"Hopefully you'll never have cause," the blonde said.

"Here's an interesting fact," Ted interjected. "Henry Ford used Spanish moss for padding the seats in the first Model Ts, but failed to boil it first. That resulted in the world's first auto recall." He laughed. "The more things change the more they stay the same."

"Ain't that the truth," the redhead said.

Alease nodded, then said, "It sure is a beautiful night to be out here."

"The temperature is just right," I said.

We sat a moment in pleasant silence as the women

continued shuffling through the mail, either dropping it in a garbage sack or piling it on the table next to them. Occasionally they would discuss one of the pieces.

Finally I said, "I guess I'll retire."

"What time will you be wanting breakfast in the morning?" Ted asked.

"What time do you serve?"

"Six to eight thirty."

"Eight would be good."

"Eight it is," he replied. "Good night."

"Good night."

"I put out some banana bread in the hallway near your room," Alease said. "It should still be warm."

"Thank you," I said.

Outside my room was a small round table with a plate of warm bread. Even though my stomach still ached a little from dinner, I took a slice. On the wall next to my door was a framed sampler that read:

> Having a place to go is a home.
> Having someone to love is a family.
> Having both is a true blessing.

I had neither. Did that make me truly *unblessed?* Cradling the bread in one hand, I unlocked the door to my room and stepped inside. I sat down on my bed and ate the bread, then pulled off my shoes, undressed, and lay down on the duvet.

I was back again. *Why? Why had I come back?* I felt like I was on the edge of the cliff about to step over. From here on my walk was due south, straight down the coast of Florida, over five hundred miles to Key West. I wasn't sure if I was up to it—emotionally or physically.

The bellow of a train's horn interrupted my thoughts. The horn was followed by the metallic clacking of a train across the rails. I wondered if the noise was something the locals ever got used to.

I sat up and took out my map to review my route. Highway 1 ran the length of the coast all the way to Key West. It seemed simple enough, but I knew from experience that my path would likely change once I hit asphalt, based on the road and the availability of hotels and restaurants. Interstate 95 also ran south and would likely provide access to both, but I always felt vulnerable walking on freeways, and in a state as populated as Florida, many stretches would be closed to pedestrians.

I traced Highway 1 down past Miami to where the keys began, at the southeastern tip of the Florida peninsula. I studied the route for just a moment, then tossed my map on the floor and lay back in bed. On the wall behind the bed was a framed sampler that read:

Faith is the bird that sings when the dawn is still dark.
—Tagore

After all this time it was hard to believe that I was actually this close. McKale and I had once talked of visiting Key West, and, had she lived, we likely would have.

I reached over and turned out the nightstand lamp, then lay listening to the train horns that blew every fifteen minutes or so. I don't know what time I fell asleep, but I didn't sleep well. I dreamed all night of oncoming trains.

CHAPTER

Twenty-Five

Usually the most interesting stories are
written not on paper but hearts.

Alan Christoffersen's diary

I woke with the sun streaming through my window. I checked my watch, and, seeing that it was a quarter after seven, I climbed into the shower. I sat on the tile floor with my head bowed, letting the water fall over me. I was feeling a little jet-lagged, but I wasn't going to let it slow me down.

I washed myself, shaved, then dressed. With the exception of what I'd worn the day before, my clothes were all clean, and I had several outfits to choose from—a luxury that wouldn't last for long. The dining room was just across the hall from my room, and as I dressed I could hear the clinking of silverware on plates.

The two women I had met the night before were sitting at the main table, joined by a man I hadn't met. He was wearing a short-sleeved Harley-Davidson shirt.

"Good morning," I said.

"Morning," they returned in a chorus. The man stood and extended his hand. "I'm William. Kelly's husband."

"I'm Kelly," the blond-haired woman said. "We didn't share names last night."

"And I'm Naomi," the redhead said.

"It's a pleasure," I said. "My name is Alan."

At the sound of my entrance, Ted emerged from the kitchen, smiling. "Good morning, Mr. Christoffersen."

"Alan," I said.

"I just like saying your last name," he replied. "Must be the pastor in me. Please, Alan, take a seat."

"May I join you?" I asked the others.

"Of course," Naomi said.

I pulled out a chair and sat down at the long table.

Ted stood at the end of the room, clasping his hands in front of him as if he were about to address a congregation. "This morning we have eggs and bacon, fruit, and homemade biscuits from scratch." He winked. "Maybe not from scratch. A pastor shouldn't lie." He looked at me. "Now, Alan, you're not from the South. Have you had grits?"

"Yes," I said. "I've walked through Tennessee, Mississippi, Alabama, and Georgia, so I've eaten a bucket of them. Maybe a wheelbarrow."

Ted laughed. "Glad to hear it. I'm especially partial to ours."

"Then I look forward to trying them."

He walked back to the kitchen.

"Did you say you walked through all those states?" William asked.

"Yes. And many more. I'm walking across America. I started in Seattle, Washington."

"Oh my," Naomi said.

"What's your profession?" William asked.

"Right now it's walking," I said.

"How does it pay?"

"It doesn't," I said. "In my former life I owned an advertising agency in Seattle."

"That explains it," William said. "Lots of money in advertising."

"There can be," I replied.

"How many miles are we from Seattle?" Naomi asked.

"Nearly three thousand," I replied.

She shook her head. "The stories you must have to tell."

"I have a few."

"Where are you headed?" William asked.

"Key West," I said.

"Key West's a little more than five hundred miles from here," William said. "You taking the Ninety-Five?"

"You can't walk the Ninety-Five," Kelly said. "It's an expressway." She turned to me. "And they've always got it tore up. Take the One—the Old Dixie Highway. It ends in Key West."

"No, he should take the A1A," Naomi said. "That'll give you the prettiest view of the ocean."

"The A1A doesn't go all the way through," William said. "He'd have to backtrack."

"I'll probably do a little of each," I said. "I've looked through my maps, but I'm sure things will change. I've learned that the maps aren't the road."

"Ain't that the truth," Kelly said.

∾

Ted and Alease's teenage daughter, Mariah, came out of the kitchen carrying a glass of orange juice. She was a pretty, tall girl wearing a yellow apron and a bright crimson blouse that seemed to glow against her smooth ebony skin. She seemed a little shy as she set the glass in front of me.

"Thank you," I said.

"You're welcome," she said, walking back to the kitchen. A moment later she returned with a bowl of fruit topped with yogurt and granola.

"Thank you," I said again.

She smiled. "You're still welcome."

I was hungry and the fruit tasted good. My table companions let me eat a moment in silence. Then William said, "Did you come down from Waycross?"

"Yes, sir."

"Did you visit the swamp?"

"I took the tour."

"The tour's better down here," Kelly said. "It's federal run. You should take it."

"I don't think I'll have the chance," I said. "I've got to get on my way."

"How far do you walk each day?" Naomi asked.

"It depends. I've gone as far as thirty miles."

"Lord, almighty," she said.

"But I usually walk around twenty to twenty-four."

"Is it dangerous?" Kelly asked.

"Of course it's dangerous," William said. "There's a lot of crazies out there." He turned to me. "I'd be carrying if I were you."

"Sometimes it's dangerous," I said. "I walked over those tracks last night. That seemed a little dangerous."

Naomi nodded. "With this many trains you've got to keep both eyes open. We've had our losses. Like Uncle George and Beth." She looked at Kelly.

Kelly frowned. "Yes, George and Beth."

"They were killed by a train?" I asked.

"About four years ago," Kelly replied.

"Darndest thing," William said, shaking his head.

"What happened?"

"They were coming back from Chucky's baptism—"

"Chucky's their grandson," Naomi said.

"It was late," Kelly said. "Their car stalled on the

tracks and George couldn't get it going again. Then he heard a train coming. He got out and went to help Beth out of the car, but she panicked and locked the door."

"They were older," Naomi said. "In their eighties."

"Beth wasn't all there," William said. "Hadn't been for years."

Naomi added, "George's friend, Marshall, was in a wheelchair across the street. He saw it all."

Kelly looked annoyed. "Will you please just let me tell the story?"

"Sorry," William said.

"I was saying, Beth locked the car door. George pled with her to open the door, but she wouldn't. Then he looked down the track at the coming train, walked back to the driver's seat, and got in."

"The train took both of them," Naomi said.

"He didn't want to go on living without her," William said. "It was tragic."

"It's tragic and beautiful at the same time," Kelly said, surrendering the story. "They got to go together."

After a moment I said, "I can understand why he would do that."

◦◦◦

Mariah came out carrying a plate with three strips of bacon, two biscuits, and scrambled eggs with cheese melted on top. Ted followed her out but stopped near the doorway, as if supervising her.

"There's blackberry jelly right there," Mariah said. "For your biscuit."

"Thank you," I said.

Ted smiled proudly. "Does everything look satisfactory?"

"Yes. Thank you. It looks delicious."

Mariah walked back into the kitchen.

"The eggs are real fresh," Ted said. "In fact, you just missed Chicken George."

"Chicken George?"

"He lives just down the street. He brings us fresh eggs every morning. Would you like some coffee?"

"Please," I said. "Thank you."

He walked back to the kitchen. I broke open a biscuit, forked some eggs inside, then folded a piece of bacon and put it inside, making a breakfast sandwich. My companions watched in silence.

I asked Kelly, "You said you're here for a funeral?"

"My brother's," Kelly said.

Sometimes, in the pain and loneliness of my losses, I forgot that I was only one of hundreds of thousands bidding their loved ones goodbye. It's like standing at the airport and not seeing anyone around you.

"Your brother lived in Folkston?" I asked.

"Just a half mile north of here," William said.

"Are you also from Folkston?" I asked.

"We live in Macon now," Kelly said.

"I've got a machine shop in Macon," William added. "Naomi lives in Jacksonville."

"How far will you walk today?" Kelly asked.

"Hopefully twenty miles. I'm breaking myself back in to walking. I went home for a few weeks, so I've gotten a little out of shape."

"I bet your family was glad to see you," Kelly said.

"There's only my father," I said. "But he passed away."

"I'm sorry," Naomi said.

"We all have our losses, don't we," Kelly said.

Ted returned with my coffee. A few minutes later

Kelly, Naomi, and William excused themselves to get ready for the funeral. I finished eating, then looked in the kitchen to thank Ted and Mariah, but they were gone. I left a five-dollar bill on the table for Mariah, then went to my room and packed.

As I was about to leave the inn, Alease and Ted walked into the foyer. Alease handed me a brown paper sack. "I put some of the banana nut bread in there," she said. "Just in case you need a snack on the way."

"You be sure to come back," Ted said. "We'll leave the light on."

"You're very kind," I said. "Thank you for everything." I stepped outside. It was time to continue my walk.

CHAPTER

Twenty-Six

Perhaps the greatest mystery of death is why
it's a mystery.

Alan Christoffersen's diary

The day was overcast and the road was wet, spotted with occasional puddles. Soon a comfortable mist filled the air—much like what I was used to in Seattle.

Walking east, I crossed the railroad tracks again. There were even more people gathered to watch the trains. After the tracks, I continued along Main Street to Second until I reached the edge of town.

Less than five miles from the inn I reached the Florida state line and the border town of Boulogne. Across the border it was easy walking along smooth, flat stretches with grassy shoulders hemmed in by a corridor of tall trees.

After two hours I reached the town of Hilliard. My legs were already sore. I walked another mile and a half, then stopped for lunch at the R&R Wings Café. I had a bowl of the Underground Chili and a half-dozen garlic honey wings, then hurried back out before my legs cramped up.

I had walked another mile when I came to a Winn-Dixie supermarket. I stopped inside for supplies, which included bottled water, canned fruit, pork and beans, protein bars, jerky, and raw almonds. I also purchased some Epsom salts to soak in later. I shopped for just half an hour, eager to keep moving.

A block from the store was a sign for the next town:

CALLAHAN 11 MILES

Callahan would put me at around twenty-two miles for the day. I thought it was a respectable goal for the first day back. I just hoped my legs had it in them to walk the whole way. As I left Hilliard the speed of the traffic increased, while mine steadily declined. I reached Callahan at around six p.m. The city sign boasted:

Home of the
FLORIDA CHEERLEADING
STATE CHAMPIONS

The first motel I came to was called the Ship Inn—a long, narrow row of rooms. The rental office was situated apart from the hotel in its own building near the road. I went in to reserve a room.

An Indian man was sitting on a mat on the floor playing a card game with a woman who was dressed in a saffron-colored sari. The office smelled of incense and curry. The man seemed annoyed that I had interrupted his game.

I got a room for just forty-five dollars. Once inside, I fell back on the bed, exhausted, my legs cramping. I lifted my legs and pulled them toward me until my hamstrings stretched. As hungry as I was, I was too tired to walk to a restaurant, so I ate Alease's banana nut bread and cold beans and fruit. Then I filled the tub with hot water and the Epsom salts and soaked until the water started to cool. That night I slept much better than I had in Folkston.

❧

The next morning as I lay in bed, I saw where someone had written on the wall:

Where will I go when I die?

My mind went back to the conversation I'd had with my father about the afterlife. I couldn't help but smile. I took a pen from the nightstand and wrote beneath the query:

Toledo

I remembered a story one of my former employees, a graphic artist named Charles, told me. He said that when he was young he'd had a cousin with leukemia. He said that one night he woke in the middle of the night to see her standing next to his bed. When he asked her what she was doing in his room she said, "Tell my mother and father that all is well." Then she was gone. The next morning his parents told him that his cousin had died in the night.

I don't know if Charles had really seen the girl or not, but I'm certain that he believed he had.

Toledo. I wondered where my father was—physically—if the word still applied. Was he walking with me? Would I even know it if he was? I thought of his dream about sitting in the garden with my mother and McKale. I hoped he was there. The thought made me feel peaceful.

I dressed, then sat down on the thinly padded carpet and again stretched my back and legs. When I felt sufficiently limber I grabbed my pack and set off for the day. It had rained during the night, and the sky was still overcast. All around me the ground and roadway were pooled with water. *Walking on water,* I thought. A mile and a half into town I reached a Huddle House restaurant. I stopped for a breakfast of blueberry pancakes.

Shortly after I left the restaurant the highway speed limit rose to sixty-five again, which affected me only because of the danger of speeding cars on wet roads. An hour later I entered Duval County and reached the Jacksonville city limit. Peculiarly, someone had hung the hoods of a dozen cars along a fence. I had no idea why. Maybe it was art.

Thirteen miles into the day I climbed the on-ramp to Interstate 295. The freeway traffic was dense and fast, at least in comparison to where I had been walking, but there were also a wide emergency lane and broad, grassy shoulders.

My legs were still not a hundred percent, so I exited the freeway short of twenty miles at Commonwealth Avenue. The shoulder was under repair, and I had to hike around barricades to get to the bottom of the off-ramp and the Comfort Suites.

There was a Wendy's drive-in adjacent to the hotel's parking lot, and I had a chicken salad, a bowl of chili, and a baked potato for dinner, then went back to my room and soaked in the last of my Epsom salts before going to bed.

⌒

The next day was stressful going. As I'd been warned back in Folkston, the expressway was "tore up" in myriad places, making it difficult to walk. At one point I was forced to climb over barricades because of road construction.

Around noon I took the Roosevelt Boulevard exit and ate lunch at one of my favorite stops, the Waffle House. I was in no hurry to return to the 95, so after lunch I tried to keep to local roads, but after an hour I could see the freeway was the only sensible route. I walked nearly five miles more, then got off on the Old St. Augustine Road.

As I descended the off-ramp I saw a sign for a Holiday Inn Express. I turned left, crossing beneath the overpass and into a well-groomed business district not a quarter mile from the exit. I had again walked less than twenty miles, but it felt like more.

The hotel shared a parking lot with a steak and seafood restaurant called LeGrand's. I lay down on my bed for about a half hour, then I got up, washed my face, and walked across the parking lot to the restaurant.

The restaurant was crowded, but, being a party of one, I was seated quickly. I had the best meal I'd had since I left California: skillet corn bread, a wedge salad, sweet potato pecan soufflé, and a twelve-ounce rib eye steak garnished with sautéed mushrooms.

There was a couple sitting just two tables away from me that I guessed to be about my age. They had a toddler, a boy, who was celebrating a birthday. The family looked so remarkably happy that I couldn't help but watch them. I surprised myself by laughing out loud when their boy smashed his hands into his piece of birthday cake. As they got up to leave, the young mother glanced over at me. I smiled. She smiled back, then turned away and pulled her child close. Suddenly, all the reasons I'd given McKale for putting off having a child seemed petty.

When I got back to the Holiday Inn I went for a

long swim, then relaxed in the hot tub until it closed around eleven.

◇

The hotel provided a free breakfast. I ate a cheese omelet with bacon and sausage, biscuits and gravy, and sticky cinnamon rolls. I went back to my room for my pack, then walked back out to the freeway.

I had walked about an hour when I exited onto the 1, which, at this part of the state, was called Philips Highway. (I was to learn that Highway 1 has more name changes than Zsa Zsa Gabor.) An hour later I passed through the town of Bayard. The skies were clearing a little, but I noticed that the shoulder to my right was filled with water, so, likely in unwarranted paranoia, I kept an eye open for gators.

Since passing the Okefenokee Swamp I'd thought a lot about alligators. There's a myth that the best way to outrun an alligator is to run zigzags, the rationale being that the reptile cannot easily adjust its path. This is wrong on two counts. First, the fastest an alligator has been recorded running is ten miles an hour, half the speed of a human sprinter and still considerably slower than any average adult can run. Second, an alligator has little endurance on land and rarely chases anything more than fifteen feet away from it. So the fastest way to put distance between you and a gator is to run in a straight line. While I realize that this information is probably useless, it does make for good conversation.

As evening fell I turned off on Palencia Village Drive and stopped at a small strip mall restaurant called Pacific Asian Bistro, where I ate edamame, miso soup, and unagi don—eel over sushi rice. After finishing my meal, I asked the proprietor, a middle-aged Chinese man, if there was a hotel in the area. He replied, "Yeah, it's close. Just keep driving another ten minutes."

Ten minutes by car was four hours by foot. I walked around the area until I finally found a clump of trees big enough to conceal my tent. I felt like I was hiding in plain sight.

CHAPTER

Twenty-Seven

Some people spend so much time hunting treasure that they fail to see it all around them. It's like sifting through gold to find the silt.

Alan Christoffersen's diary

I didn't sleep well. I woke early, broke down my tent, and walked back out to Highway 1. I wasn't too concerned with my lack of sleep, since I planned to walk for only a few hours anyway. The city of St. Augustine was only seven miles away, and I wanted to spend some time there.

St. Augustine is America's oldest European-settled city. It was founded more than two centuries before the Declaration of Independence was signed and served as the capital of Spanish Florida for over two hundred years. The town, like most of early America, has a bloody past, and control of the region has changed hands multiple times. It was first colonized by the French, then seized by the Spanish and traded to the British.

A quarter mile into the town was a parking lot and booth with a sign that read:

Old Town Trolley Tours

I purchased a ticket and waited for the next trolley to arrive. Tourism was light that day, and I took an entire bench on the trolley for myself and my pack, behind a family I deduced was from Kansas from their Jayhawks sweatshirts.

It was pleasant sitting on the trolley as it wound through the city's historic streets accompanied by the driver's commentary. The trolley ticket was an all-day pass, so I got off in the old town near Aviles Street, the oldest street in America, walked around awhile, then reboarded and crossed the Bridge of Lions to Anastasia Island, where I took a tour of the St. Augustine Alligator Farm, which, for a reptile lover like myself, was well worth the admission.

The park had all twenty-three living species of crocodilians, the most interesting being the gharial, with its long, toothy snout as narrow as a French baguette.

In the center of the park was a pool filled with some of the largest alligators I had ever seen. They were monsters, motionless as statues. They were obviously well fed, because during a feeding demonstration a dead chicken landed on one of the alligators' heads and it was still there when I left ten minutes later.

After the farm, I walked over to the St. Augustine Lighthouse, 140 years old and striped white and black like a giant, monochromatic barber pole. I checked my pack at the front registry, then walked through the lighthouse keeper's house (which had been converted into a museum), then to the lighthouse.

McKale loved lighthouses, and I thought of her as I climbed the 219 steps to the deck on top.

I had been warned by the ticket taker to remove my hat before I reached the top, and the reason became obvious as I walked out on the deck. The sea winds were powerful enough to remove hats and sunglasses.

The deck provided a 360-degree view of St. Augustine, the Intracoastal Waterway, and the Atlantic Ocean.

I climbed back down the lighthouse and caught the trolley to the mainland. I asked the driver about a good restaurant, and he recommended Meehan's Irish Pub & Seafood House, which was near one of his stops.

Even though it was the town's off-season, the restaurant was crowded. The hostess, a pretty young blond woman with a (I hoped temporary) shamrock tattoo on her cheek, informed me that there was a twenty-five-minute wait for a table unless I wanted to eat at the bar, which I elected to do.

I sat at the end of the bar, where I could keep an eye on my pack, and perused the menu. The pub's motto was "Eat, Drink, and be Irish," so I ordered their Irish specials: a Reuben roll (which was something like an Asian spring roll but was filled with corned beef and sauerkraut), conch chowder, and shepherd's pie.

I was finishing my meal when a man sat down next to me. He was probably a little older than my father, tan with sun-spotted, leathery skin. His blond hair was streaked with gray and pulled back in a ponytail. He wore a Tommy Bahama flowered shirt and cargo shorts. He glanced over at me and nodded his head a little.

"Evening," I said.

"Evening," he replied.

He ordered a beer and shepherd's pie. He glanced past me at my pack, then asked, "Passing through town?"

I nodded. "I'm headed to Key West."

"Good place to be headed," he said. "I'm Gaspar." He extended his hand.

"Alan," I replied. "Gaspar. That's an unusual name."

"Not so unusual around here," he said.

"So you're from here," I said.

"I was born near Vero, but I've lived here for the last twenty-six years. You?"

"Born in Denver, raised in Pasadena. But I moved to Seattle for work."

"What do you do?"

"I used to be in advertising," I said. "Now I just walk."

"There's a profession. Are you paid by the mile or the hour? Actually, a better question is *who* pays you? And why?"

"It's pro bono," I said.

He grinned. "Why wouldn't it be?"

"What do you do?" I asked.

"I'm a treasure hunter."

"Really. What kind of treasure do you hunt?"

"Buried, mostly."

"You've found buried treasure?"

"Some. The big one's eluded me, but I'll find it some-day. It's just a matter of time."

"There's a lot of treasure around here?"

"Florida has more lost treasure than anywhere else in the world, and only a fraction of it's been found. A few years back road crews were building a road in Brevard County and unearthed thirteen chests of coins.

"Every now and then Spanish doubloons and pieces of eight from shipwrecks will wash up on the beaches after heavy storms, but most of the loot was buried on land by pirates."

"Pirates?"

"These waters were full of them. Captain Morgan, of the rum fame, Calico Jack, Black Caesar, and the most famous, José Gaspar. My namesake."

"I've never heard of Gaspar," I said. "But I'm not much on piratology." I wasn't sure that was a word.

The bartender returned with Gaspar's food and drink. In one swig Gaspar downed a quarter of his mug, then wiped the foam from his mouth and turned back to me.

"Gaspar's big in Florida. There's a Gasparilla celebration in Tampa every year."

"Why would they celebrate a thief?" I asked.

"We celebrate worse," he said. "Columbus wiped out thousands of indigenous peoples, and we have a holiday for him. It all depends on how you view it. To some, Captain Morgan was a pirate, but he preyed on enemies of Britain, so he was knighted by the British Crown. One man's hero is another man's criminal."

"Gaspar too?" I asked.

"No, he was pretty much in it for himself. He was just born bad, I guess. He committed his first crime at the age of twelve. He kidnapped a girl and held her for ransom. Being so young, he was easily caught. He was given the option of prison or the Spanish navy. He chose the sea.

"Apparently Gaspar was quite handsome. When he was older he was involved in a love affair with the king's daughter, until he was accused of stealing the royal crown jewels. Before he could be arrested, he fled Spain, then, supposedly with the money from the jewels, purchased a ship and crew, sailed to the Florida coast, and began attacking any ship flying the Spanish flag. It's believed that he attacked more than four hundred ships, including the vessel carrying the twelve million dollars in gold bullion that the United States paid Napoleon for the Louisiana Purchase. Some of the gold was lost at sea, but most of it was buried."

"How do you know that?"

"I feel it," he said, pounding his chest. "In here." He took another drink, then said, "Every now and then there's a story that confirms it. Just before the Revolutionary War, one of Gaspar's last living confederates came out of hiding. He asked a farmer for his help in recovering the gold, promising him a share of the booty. The farmer was doubtful but decided to help out the old man. After they raised the first chest, he was pretty eager to continue. But the old man said he wasn't feeling well and needed a few days' rest. Two days later the farmer went to see him and found him dead in his cabin. The farmer went through the cabin, and all he found was a jar of gold coins and a code he had engraved in copper." Gaspar reached into his pocket and brought out a piece of paper.

"I carry this with me wherever I go. It's a Xerox of a pencil rubbing from that sheet of copper."

O-X-NXW-W-VER-VAR
LEGUA 1/10 O-X-SWXW-VER-VAR
HASTA X

"I've been trying to decipher it for twenty-six years now."

"You've spent half your life searching for treasure?"

"At least."

"What did you do before that?"

"I drove a truck. Before that I took people on tours of St. Augustine. That's where I learned so much about the history of this place."

"Are you married?"

He took another long drink, pounding his glass down with a loud thud. "No. I planned to get married, have a family, the usual, but after I found treasure, time just sort of slipped away."

I nodded.

"How about you?"

"I was married."

"Was?"

"She passed away a year ago."

"I'm sorry to hear that."

I took a drink of my beer, then said, "She was my treasure."

He looked at me for a moment, then turned and drained the rest of his mug. He had nothing else to say.

CHAPTER

Twenty-Eight

What was true three thousand years ago is true today: the end of the siren's song is death.

Alan Christoffersen's diary

I got a late start the next day, leaving my motel around noon. I followed Ponce de Leon to US 1 to 95 south, into Flagler County. If you travel through Florida, it's impossible not to see the name Flagler. Henry Morrison Flagler was a railroad and oil tycoon and a founding partner, along with John D. Rockefeller, of Standard Oil.

By 1896 his railroad, the Florida East Coast Railway, reached all the way south to Biscayne Bay, where he dredged a channel, built streets and utilities, and even founded the first newspaper.

The grateful locals wanted to name the city Flagler, but he declined the offer. Instead he convinced them to use an Indian name, Mayaimi, later shorted to Miami. It was a good call. Somehow the Flagler Dolphins doesn't have the same ring to it.

I stayed overnight in Palm Coast at a Microtel Inn & Suites, then set out again the next day. Interstate 95 met up with Highway 1, which again changed names, this time to Dixie Highway. I walked through Volusia County to Ormond Beach, then, as the sun set, into the city of Daytona Beach. It was nearly dark when I reached a city sign that read:

Welcome to Daytona Beach

Walking on Water

Ten yards after it was another sign that read:

We're glad you're back.
Please keep the noise down.

I walked over a bridge and east until a neon sign stretched across the road.

World's Most Famous Beach

December is the off-season in Daytona—a lull before the hordes descend in February for the Daytona 500. Still, there was less traffic in the city than I expected.

As I walked toward the ocean I heard reggae music playing. After a dull day of walking, I liked the idea of losing myself in the party atmosphere, so I walked past the beachfront buildings to investigate.

The music was coming from an outdoor bar called Il Galli, and the sign in front had a picture of a rooster. The crowded bar had a fire pit in the middle of the bricked terrace—the flickering, orange-yellow flames illuminating the band. I walked up to a hostess, who glanced up as I approached.

"Do you have a table?" I asked.

She nodded. "Yes, are you alone?"

"Yes," I said.

She grabbed a menu from the hostess stand, then said flippantly, "Not for long."

I followed her to the far side of the bar near the band, whose music seemed to be increasing in volume.

As I looked through the menu, a waitress walked up to me. She almost had to shout to be heard over the music. "What can I get you to drink?"

"Just a beer," I said.

"What kind would you like?"

"What's this Dark Lord Russian?"

"It's a local brew. It's popular. It has the taste of coffee and molasses. It's a little pricey, but most say it's worth it."

"I'll try it."

"I don't think you'll be disappointed. Do you want anything to eat?"

"I'll have one of your pulled pork sandwiches. With Swiss cheese and coleslaw."

"Fries or chips?"

"Fries. And a side Caesar salad."

"You got it."

I sat back in my chair. It felt good to be off my feet. The weather was nice, and the air was sweet and moist with the ocean breeze.

The band's main singer and drummer wore dreadlocks. They weren't Bob Marley and the Wailers, and I suspected that what they lacked in talent they tried to make up for in volume. I tore off a couple pieces of napkin, rolled them into marble-sized balls, and put them in my ears.

The people around me were mostly younger. With the exception of a few older men sitting at the bar, I was the only one alone—something that wasn't new to me, but in this kind of setting it made me feel self-conscious.

Sitting at the far end of the bar were two women, likely in their late twenties, one blond, the other brunette. The blonde had a petite build and wore a black string bikini with a sheer cover-up that didn't cover up much. The other woman, a tan brunette, was slightly taller and voluptuous. She was wearing turquoise shortshorts, frayed at the bottom, with an orange bikini top.

They were both gorgeous, a fact that wasn't lost on the men around them, who were almost all gawking at them or at least stealing glances—some more obvious than others.

The brunette looked a little like Falene, which intensified my loneliness. The truth is, seeing them reminded me that I wasn't wired to be celibate.

The brunette looked at me and smiled. I smiled back, expecting her to turn away, but she didn't. She continued staring at me, her eyes dark and piercing. Her friend noticed her gaze and looked at me as well and smiled. She waved me over, but I just smiled. She turned back to the barkeep and said something, smiled at me again, then turned away. A moment later a waiter brought me a beer.

"You're a lucky man. This is from the ladies at the end of the bar," he said, glancing back at my benefactors. "They would like you to join them."

I followed his gaze over to the women. They were both smiling at me. The blonde cocked her head and raised her eyebrows.

"All right," I finally said. I pulled the extemporaneous earplugs from my ears, then, leaving my pack at the table, picked up my beer and carried it over to the women. They both preened a little as I neared. They were even prettier up close. To tell the truth, I wasn't used to this kind of thing and I felt a little awkward.

"Thanks for the beer," I said, setting it on the counter.

"You're welcome," the brunette said.

"I'm Alan," I said.

"I'm Lindsi," the blonde replied, reaching out her hand. I took it. Gathered at her wrists were clumps of gold and silver bracelets. Her hair fell to her shoulders except for a single braid that lay to the side of her face. She had on bright red lipstick that accentuated her full lips. She wore a long gold chain that was tied together above her cleavage and fell to her taut stomach.

"And I'm Renny," the brunette said. I thought she was even more striking than Lindsi. Her eyes were amber-brown and almond shaped above high cheekbones. She had a tattoo of a mermaid on her shoulder. She looked even more like Falene up close.

"Renny," I said. "That's a different name."

She just smiled. I doubted she'd heard me.

"First time here?" Lindsi asked.

I moved closer to them so they could hear. "It's my first time in Daytona," I said. "I'm just passing through."

"Where are you headed?" Renny asked.

"Key West."

"Key West is wild," Lindsi said. "It's like a big, twenty-four-seven freak party."

"The last time I was there," Renny said, "I got so drunk, I woke up on the beach with a chicken pecking at my earring."

"They've got chickens all over down there," Lindsi said. "It's crazy."

"Hunter Thompson said, 'Key West is where the weird go pro,'" I said.

"What?" Renny said.

Just then the band ended a song, leaving my ears ringing.

"Hunter Thompson said that 'Key West is where the weird go pro.'"

"Who?" Lindsi said.

"Hunter Thompson. The writer."

Renny rolled her eyes. "Lindsi's not much on reading."

"Like you are," Lindsi said.

Renny looked at me. "I'm into . . . other things." Her smile grew. "Where are you from, Alan?"

"Seattle."

"I've been to Seattle," she said. "I have some friends there. You're a long way from home."

"Other side of the continent."

"What brings you to our side?" Lindsi asked.

"Just seeing the country."

"Where are you staying in Daytona?" Lindsi asked.

"In a hotel."

"Which one?"

"I haven't found one yet."

"You can stay at our place," Lindsi said. "It's not far from here. Why don't you come back with us for a few drinks and . . . whatever?"

They both looked at me intently.

"Thanks, but . . ."

Renny brought out a small baggie from her bikini top. There were pills inside. "I've got *candy*."

I just looked at them.

"Come on," Lindsi said. "It will be fun. I promise."

"I don't . . ."

Lindsi smiled, moving her hand to my thigh. "You don't what?"

"I'm married," I said.

Lindsi looked at me skeptically. "I don't see a ring."

"I don't see a wife," Renny said. "Did you lose her?"

"Finders keepers," Lindsi said playfully.

Renny slid forward on her stool. Smiling seductively, she put her hand on my arm. "Come on. Let's have some fun."

"Really, I . . ."

"Come on," Lindsi said, taking my hand.

I pulled my hand away from her. "No."

Lindsi's smile vanished. "What's wrong with you?"

"I told you, I'm married."

"Then why'd you come over and hit on us?" she asked.

I looked at them a moment, then said, "You bought me a drink."

"You came over because you liked what you saw," Lindsi said.

"What's the matter?" Renny asked. "Are you afraid of us?"

I picked up my beer. "I'm *afraid* I've given you the wrong impression. I'm sorry to waste your time."

I turned and walked away.

"Loser," Renny said, loud enough for half the bar to hear.

I walked back to my table and sat down. A moment later I glanced back at the women. They had already walked over to a table of men. My waitress brought my sandwich and beer.

"Here you go." She set the plate before me. "One pulled pork sandwich and . . . another Dark Lord."

"Thanks."

"Anything else?"

"Just the check."

"I'll be right back." She hesitated for a moment, then said, "For the record, you made the right choice." She turned and walked away.

When she returned with my check I said, "What do you mean I made the right choice?"

"Those two girls, Lindsi and Renny. They're bad news. They've sunk more men than the barrier reef."

"Sunk?"

"Hearts, marriages, bank accounts, souls. Pick one." She smiled. "You're one of the smart ones."

In light of the humiliation the girls had just flung at me, it was good to hear this. "Thank you."

"Thank yourself," she said, then turned and walked away.

A few minutes later I looked back over to where the women had been standing, but they, and the men, were already gone.

I finished eating, drank just one of the beers, then grabbed my pack and walked back out to the frontage road. I walked a quarter mile more before finding a hotel. For one of the few times since I'd left Seattle, I was glad to be alone.

∽

I got up early the next morning and went for a short walk along the beach. In Daytona, cars are allowed to drive on the beach, and as I walked a dozen or so vintage Corvettes passed by.

I ate breakfast at the hotel, which I realized catered to the elderly, as I was the only one in the dining room under seventy. The complimentary meal included runny eggs, chipped beef, and Cream of Wheat. When several of the women began taking an overt interest in me, I grabbed my pack and left.

About a half hour later I walked past the famous Daytona Beach Drive-In Christian Church, where you come as you are, tune your radio to 680 AM or 88.5 FM, and hear God's word. I had to smile. It was a far cry from what McKale and I used to do in drive-ins.

∽

The next three days were peaceful and, frankly, not worth writing about. My walk took me through New Smyrna Beach, Edgewater, Oak Hill, and then to Titusville, aka Space City, USA. I entered the town, walking past Astronaut High School. I found a room at the Budget Motel, paying forty-five dollars to a smiling, toothless woman at the front desk, ate dinner next door at the Your Place Restaurant, then went to my room and crashed. I felt like I was coming down with something.

CHAPTER

Twenty-Nine

Humanity is always looking for the next great world, the next frontier. I wonder how different this world would be if we were content with where we were.

Alan Christoffersen's diary

I woke sick. I wasn't coughing, fortunately, but I felt feverish and achy, so I decided to rest for a day—which, frankly, I was planning on doing anyway so I could tour the nearby Kennedy Space Center. I ate breakfast at the restaurant next door, then walked a block to a drugstore, where I purchased some cold-relief capsules. Then I took a cab to the space center on Merritt Island.

My father was fascinated by space travel. I'll always remember the look on his face as he told me about watching the *Apollo 11* moon landing in July 1969, repeating Neil Armstrong's words, "That's one small step for man, one giant leap for mankind." My father told me that Armstrong had not only prepared the speech himself *after* landing on the moon but had unintentionally dropped the word *a* before *man*, which technically changed the quote's meaning.

When I was twelve my father took me to see an actual moon rock at the California Science Center, and for the next week I drank nothing but orange-flavored Tang, the drink of astronauts. Most interesting to me were the exhibits and museums that displayed actual artifacts from space history, including the original Mercury mission control consoles, and the Rocket Garden—an exhibit of the actual Mercury-Redstone, Atlas, and Titan rockets that the first astronauts rode into space. There were also the Mercury, Gemini, and Apollo capsules.

Seeing the space center made me miss my father.

The space center closed at five p.m., so I called a taxi to take me back to the hotel. I was still feeling crummy, so I ate a light dinner at Your Place Restaurant, then went to bed before nine.

∽

Fortunately, I woke feeling better. I got an early start, walking US 1 through Bellwood, Delespine, Port St. John, Frontenac, Williams Point, and Sharpes, stopping for the night at a hotel on Merritt Island.

The next day I took SR 520 east until I reached SR A1A south, which took me through the south end of Merritt Island and Cocoa Beach, past Patrick Air Force Base, home of the 45th Space Wing, assigned to NASA and outer space. As I passed the base's entrance I felt a twinge of anxiety. The last time I had passed an air force base was just outside of Spokane, the night I was stabbed.

I had sporadically encountered long stretches of road-kill in the Midwest, but that was nothing compared to the A1A, where I saw more run-over animals than anywhere else on my walk. Except on this side of the continent the deceased creatures were crustaceans. Crabs—thousands of them smashed and baked into the pavement. Outside of Orchid Island I had to watch my step, as there were plenty of them still alive, running sideways in waves across the asphalt splattered with their brethren. I had no idea what motivated them on their suicidal trek, but I did make a bad joke about it.

Why did the crab cross the road?
To get to the other—*Crunch*.

～

Two days later I reached Vero Beach at around two thirty in the afternoon. Vero Beach is one of the wealthiest cities in Florida, evidenced by a plethora of boutiques and art galleries.

As I entered the town I stopped at the Village Beach Market. I purchased some food, then asked Marge, a pleasant, lavender-haired woman at the checkout counter, about the area. She told me that the bulk of the hotels were spread out over the next two miles along the beach. After that I would encounter miles of condominiums and gated residences.

It would be only four by the time I reached the beach, which was earlier than I usually stopped but too late to make it to the next city. I knew from experience that it was difficult to camp in residential areas, particularly an upscale one like Vero Beach, which meant my best bet would be to find a hotel nearby. Marge recommended that I stay at the Driftwood Resort.

I sat on the grass in front of the store and ate a lunch of pineapple cucumber juice, a tuna wrap, and spears of freshly cut pineapple. Then I walked down Mango Road toward the beach until I reached Ocean Drive. I had walked about a mile when I reached the Driftwood Resort.

The Driftwood is a rustic-looking place, and is listed on the National Register of Historic Places. It was built in the early 1900s with cypress logs and cypress paneling cut from the swamps around the Blue Cypress Lake, about twenty-five miles away. Parts of the building were constructed without plans, which, considering the vernacular architecture, wasn't hard to believe. Scattered around the grounds was an eclectic collection of memorabilia ranging from captains' wheels to ship bells—one of which was said to have been owned by Harriet Beecher Stowe.

I told the woman at the registration counter that Marge at the Village Beach Market had recommended I stay there, so she gave me a deal on their last room, a cottage about fifty feet from the lobby.

There was a hand-painted wooden sign above the room's entrance with a picture of a large fish, which I assumed was a tarpon, since my room was named the Tarpon Cottage.

I went inside and took a long nap. I woke after dark, started the water in the jetted tub, and lay back down on the bed. Unfortunately, the hot water ran out long before the tub was filled, so I skipped the bath and went to dinner instead at the hotel restaurant, Waldo's, which claimed to be "The Last of the Great American Hangouts."

The food was good. I ordered crab cakes, peel-and-eat shrimp, and Bermuda triangles, which I followed with "Crazy Harry's" Cobb salad. I never asked who Harry was or why he was crazy.

There was a band playing near the pool in back, so after I finished eating I went outside to listen as the moon rose above the Atlantic. After a while, the crowds around the pool made me feel lonely, so I went back to my room and turned on the television. There was a football game on—the Seattle Seahawks and the Miami Dolphins. I watched the game for only a quarter, then turned off the television and went to bed.

CHAPTER

Thirty

To deny our pasts is to burn the bridge we
must cross to self-understanding.

Alan Christoffersen's diary

From my room I watched the sun rise from the horizon, turning the sky a beautiful rose-gold hue, then pure gold.

I emerged from my room feeling refreshed and rested. The Atlantic air was already humid and sweet, smelling of the perfume of flowers I couldn't name and hadn't ever smelled in the West.

I returned my room key to the front office, then headed off, walking south along Ocean Drive. Ocean Drive turned west onto Club Drive, which led me through a residential area as thick and tangled as a jungle. It was like walking through a labyrinth, and I had to retrace my steps twice, setting me back at least twenty minutes. I finally emerged from the neighborhood, crossed a bridge, then headed south through Fort Pierce, walking past beautiful golf courses and lush landscapes.

I noticed that in Vero Beach many of the streets were named after flowers, but in Fort Pierce the roads had nautical names, like Sea Mist, Oyster Bay, and Harbor Lane.

For more than an hour I walked along the beach listening to a soundtrack of screeching gulls, the crashing ocean, and the singing of cicadas. The noon sun was hot, but it was mercifully tempered by the ocean's breeze.

Fort Pierce is the place of origin of the Navy SEALs, and I passed the National Navy UDT-SEAL Museum before Highway A1A turned west into Shorewinds Drive and Fort Pierce. I crossed a drawbridge over the Indian River, followed the Old Dixie Highway to the next inter-section, where it turned into US 1, then walked another ten miles before calling it a day.

As the sun fell, I booked a room at the Days Inn. The man at the front desk recommended I eat dinner at a place about two blocks from the hotel called Lottie's Eats. I took my pack to the room, then went out looking for the restaurant. It turned out to be one of the strangest stops of my entire walk.

❧

From the road, the restaurant looked deserted, and if it weren't for the hotel clerk's directions I probably would have just walked on by without noticing it. A carved wood sign above the door read LOTTIE'S EATS, the words framed with sharp-petaled flowers of alternating pink and white. The door squeaked on its hinges as I pushed it open.

The room had a dingy, bar-like atmosphere, with peeling tile floors and a half-dozen round tables, some with cloths, some without. The place was empty except for four men who sat at one of the tables in the corner, their eyes glued to a television mounted to the wall. They were watching a football game. Their table was clut-tered with mostly empty bottles and mugs and a bowl of pretzels.

As I walked in, all of the men turned and looked at me, which might have been intimidating, but it wasn't. They looked slightly inebriated and happy to see me.

"Welcome," one of the men said, lifting a beer bottle. "C'mon in."

"Thank you." I couldn't tell if the men were customers or restaurant staff, but, as there appeared to be no one else in the restaurant, I decided on the latter. "Can I get something to eat?" I asked. Even though the sign out front read EATS, it wasn't immediately clear to me that the place served food.

"Course," the man said. He turned to one of the others, a curly-topped man with a boyish face. "Leonard, get him a menu and something to drink."

The man pushed his chair back. "What are you drinking?" he asked.

"Just water," I said.

"You can join us over here," the first man said.

"Thank you." I walked over to the table and sat down.

"You got a name?" he asked.

"Alan."

"I'm Lottie," he replied.

"You're Lottie," I said. "So you own this place."

"She owns me," he said. "This here is Otis and Troy."

The two men looked at me with half-shuttered eyes, their heads bobbing over mostly full glasses of amber liquid.

"Hi," I said.

"Hey," said Troy. Otis looked too drunk to talk. The lanky man returned with my water and a menu.

"And that's Leonard."

"Hey," he said, sitting back down.

"Where you coming from?" Lottie asked.

"Seattle." I looked at him. "Usually, people ask where I'm going."

"What's the point of that?" Lottie said. "Where you going ain't nothing." He lifted his glass. "Look at Leonard here. When he came to us he was headed somewhere." He paused. "Where was you headed?"

"Don't remember," Leonard said, his brow furrowing beneath the weight of the question.

"He left his home and just never went back."

Leonard rubbed his chin. "I think it was a couple a years ago. Maybe it was just last Christmas. I'm sure the house is gone by now. Probably someone I don't even know sleepin' in my bed."

"Probably some guy sleepin' with your *wife* in your bed," Troy said.

"Probably," Leonard replied matter-of-factly. "She's somebody else's problem now." He laughed, and all three men joined him.

I suddenly realized who the men reminded me of—Steinbeck's Mack and the boys from *Cannery Row*. I looked over the menu. "What's good?"

"We've got buffalo wings and the Lottie's Burger," Lottie said.

I wasn't sure if he was recommending those things or if they were all they had. "Sounds good," I said.

"You heard him," Lottie said to Leonard. Leonard stood and walked to the kitchen.

"Troy, get Alan a beer. The special."

"I'm okay," I said.

"Didn't say you weren't," Lottie said.

Troy staggered over to the bar, returning a moment later with a foaming mug of beer.

"House draft," Lottie said. "Courtesy of the house."

"Thank you," I said.

"Try it," he said.

Not wanting to offend my host, I took a drink. It was different from anything I'd ever tasted. Strong.

"What is this?"

"Specialite de la maison. I call it Lottie's Brew." He looked at me. "Drink up."

Stupidly, I took another drink. It burned.

"Why are you here?" Lottie asked.

My face felt hot. "The guy at the hotel recommended you."

"I mean *not* in Seattle."

"I'm walking."

He looked at me with an odd expression, then said, "Drink some more."

I'm not sure why, but I again lifted the glass. There was buzzing in my ears. I've always been able to handle my drinks, but after just a few gulps of his "brew" I was feeling fuzzy. Or drugged.

After a moment I said, "I better go."

"Your food hasn't come out yet," Lottie said.

I took out my wallet. "It's okay, I'll pay. I just need to go."

"Need?" Lottie said. "Everything a man needs is right here. Why are you walking, anyway?"

I rubbed my face. "What?"

"I asked, why are you walking?"

"I don't know."

Lottie nodded. "Like most of humanity, out looking for something that's ultimately not worth finding. I've been there, the corporate grinding stone. You know what grinding stones make? Powder."

"They make flour," Troy said.

Lottie slapped him on the head. "What's flour, moron? It's wheat powder—like your mealy brain. That's all men are today, powder. Except us." He eyed me carefully. "I bet there's a woman tangled up in this."

I took a deep breath. "My wife—"

Lottie clapped his hands. "Was I right, boys?"

"You called it," Troy said.

Otis grunted.

"Women are just another grinding stone. We got everything we need right here. Beer, television, lively conversation."

"Where'd you say you're headed?" Otis asked, surprising me that he could speak.

"He didn't," Lottie said.

"Key West," I said.

"What you lookin' for in Key West?" Troy asked.

Even without the buzz I'm not sure I could have answered the question.

Just then Leonard walked out with my food. He set the plates in front of me, then sat back down at the table. With the way I was feeling, the sight of the food made me want to throw up.

"I'll tell you what's in Key West," Lottie said. "Some good booze, but nothing worth the walk." He leaned forward. "I've never done this before, but I'm inviting you to join us. Right here, right now. We've got a spare room in the back. You can help out around the place to earn your board."

I felt the room spinning. "That's generous," I said. "But no thank you."

"No?" Lottie looked offended. "What are you holding on to?"

"I had a wife . . ."

"Had?"

"She's gone."

"Exactly. They all up and leave."

"She didn't leave me. She died."

"What's the difference?" Lottie said. "Either way she's

gone and you're alone." He looked into my eyes. "Why are you really walking? Do you even know?"

I couldn't think.

"What you looking for, Alan?"

"Hope," I said.

He burst out laughing. "Hope? Thank goodness you haven't found it. Hope was the worst thing to come out of Pandora's box. Hope is what tortures us. It's what keeps us driving the nails deeper into our palms. You want happiness, then let hope go. Let it all go—forget the past. It's nothing but regret and pain."

I had to force myself to speak. "To forget the past is to erase ourselves," I said.

"Well said," Leonard said.

"Exactly," Lottie said. "We are the great erased." He raised his glass. "And this is the great eraser."

"You can't erase the past," I said.

"You're wrong," Lottie said. "Just look at Leonard. He has no past."

Leonard grinned. "I'd rather have a bottle in front of me than a frontal lobotomy."

The men laughed.

"It eventually catches up," I said. "The past is hunting us."

"You're right," Lottie said. "You can't outrun the past. But you can kill it. Some things should be killed. It's the memories that bring pain. Only an idiot would choose pain over pleasure."

"Life *is* pain," I said.

Lottie grinned. "What are you, a Buddhist monk?"

"He's one of those gimps," Otis said. "He likes the pain."

"It's our memories that make us who we are," I said. "Killing them is a betrayal of life."

"He's talking gibberish," Troy said.

"No. I'm not." I stood up, my knees wobbly. "I've got to go."

"You go out there," Lottie said, pointing to the door, "and your past will find you. I promise you that."

"The past finds everyone," I said. "Even you. Even in here."

He lifted his beer. "Not in here it won't. In here we drown it with my brew."

"You're wrong," I said. "The past floats."

I turned and staggered out of the bar.

CHAPTER

Thirty-One

I've wondered why the famous congregate
with each other. Perhaps it's to assure each
other that they really are as important as
they think they are.

Alan Christoffersen's diary

I woke the next morning with a throbbing headache. I didn't even remember walking back to my hotel. I wondered what Lottie put in his "brew."

After throwing up, I took a long shower, then went downstairs to the hotel's breakfast nook. I drank two strong cups of black coffee and ate some oatmeal and toast before I headed out on US 1 through the commercial section of Port St. Lucie.

Around noon I was feeling human again. I stopped at a Walmart to stock up on supplies. I walked past a faded Volkswagen Jetta with a bumper sticker that read:

I'M NOT ANTISOCIAL.
I'M JUST NOT USER FRIENDLY.

I got the usual supplies, including water and disposable razors. I walked another mile south, then stopped to eat lunch at the Original Pancake House. I've always been a fan of pancakes, and the Original Pancake House has some of the best. I had Swedish pancakes with powdered sugar and lingonberries.

Next I walked through Jensen Beach, passing myriad red and yellow signs marking turtle nesting areas. Around twilight I reached the town of Hobe Sound. I couldn't see any hotels, so I stopped at Twin Rivers RV Park to see if

I could camp there. A sign directed me to a small trailer home. I knocked on the door. A voice shouted out, "Be right there." A moment later the door opened and a man stepped out. He wore a faded blue T-shirt printed with a picture of a marlin.

"What can I do for you?"

"Do you allow campers?"

"Of course. We've got lots of campers. Also RVs and trailer homes."

"I mean just with a tent."

"Just you? Sure, I've got a place near the back. Need hookups?"

I wondered what he was thinking I'd need hookups for. "No, I just need a place to stake my tent. Do you have showers and a restroom?"

"Yes. We've got a full clubhouse with showers, a pool table, and a dartboard. And a washer and dryer."

"Perfect," I said. I got out my wallet. "How much?"

He had to think about it. "Hmm. Twenty."

I handed him two tens. "How do you pronounce the name of this city?"

"Hobe," he replied. "Like *hope* but with a *b*. People up north always say Ho-bee, like it's got a *y* on the end. Where are you from?"

"Seattle."

"Do tell. My wife's from the Seattle area. Renton."

"I had some employees from Renton," I said. "I lived in Bridle Trails. Near Bellevue."

"I've been there," he said, nodding. "Nice area. Wealthy. If you want to see some real wealth, go up ahead a bit and turn left on Bridge Road. There's a bunch of celebrities that live up there. Tiger Woods lives there. At least he did; I'm not sure if he's still there—after all that ruckus in the media—but there's a bunch of them. Alan Jackson, Celine Dion, a few supermodels, Burt Reynolds . . . You should see it."

I thought it a little peculiar that he seemed so proud of the wealthy area when he lived in an RV park.

"Thanks for the tip," I said. "Maybe I'll check it out."

He picked up a map from a patio table near the trailer's door, marked an X on it, and handed it to me. "You're right there," he said. "In back, right across from the club."

"Thanks," I said.

"Have a good night."

It was clear that many of the residents had been there for a while, as there were satellite dishes, barbecue grills, even a few gardens. There was a small swimming pool, but it was plastered with signs saying that it wasn't open to RV residents.

I set up my tent, then went to wash my clothes, but there were only two washing machines and they were both in use. I took a shower and shot some pool before going back to my tent to sleep.

Maybe it was the park owner's talk of models on Jupiter Island, but as I lay in my tent my thoughts drifted to Falene. I had been so surprised when she told me that she was getting married that I hadn't even asked her when. For all I knew, she already was. At that moment I recalled the Pentecostal pastor I had stayed with in Pevely, Missouri. He had seen a vision of Falene in a wedding gown. I guess I had just assumed that it would be my wedding too.

◆

The next morning I ate breakfast from my pack. The park manager's excitement over Jupiter Island had made me a little curious, so I decided to check it out. I took the turn-off to the island, and the road led me over a small bridge, then through a tunnel of trees.

I walked around the island for a while. It was an interesting detour but definitely not what I had expected. There were no huge gated homes or spacious mansions with long driveways. In fact, the homes looked surprisingly normal.

The area was not easy to navigate, and I ended up walking in a circle back to the same road I'd entered from. Returning to US 1, I passed Burt Reynolds Park, followed by massive road construction. I ended my day at a Hampton Inn in Juno Beach and ate dinner at the Juno Beach Fish House.

⌒

The next two days I logged nearly forty-three miles, passing through the upscale city of Boca Raton, announced by its luxury car dealerships, plastic surgery offices, and funeral homes.

I had always thought that the name Boca Raton meant "rat's mouth" in Spanish, an odd name for such a wealthy area, but I was wrong on several counts. In Spanish *ratón* means "mouse," not "rat"—but the name of the city doesn't mean that either. In nautical terms, *boca* refers to an inlet. And *ratones* in old Spanish maritime dictionaries refers to rugged or stony ground. So the name basically means "rocky inlet."

Wealthy city or not, I lived economically that night. I booked a room at a Comfort Inn just a few blocks from the ocean and ate dinner at the Subway sandwich shop next door.

The next morning I ate the hotel's complimentary breakfast, then I donned my pack and walked east over the bridge to US 1.

I was able to walk on sidewalks for most of the day until I reached Fort Lauderdale, made famous by the hordes of college students that overran the town every spring break. As I reached the city I wasn't feeling all that tired, so I decided to push on to the next city: Hollywood.

Hollywood is a resort town, beautifully landscaped and aesthetically pleasing. Even the town's water tower, above Hallandale Beach, was painted to look like a giant beach ball.

I walked along Hallandale Beach Boulevard, then followed Ocean Drive north until I came to the luxurious Westin Diplomat Resort & Spa. I decided to live a little, so I booked a room, which was available only because of a last-minute cancellation.

After dinner I changed into my swimsuit and went down to the pool area to soak in the hot tub. The sun had set, and the air was moist with the ocean's cool, dark breath.

In the midst of the luxurious setting I was more troubled than I had been for months. Oddly, I wasn't sure why. At first I blamed my anxiety on the usual suspects: McKale's and my father's deaths, and Falene's rejection. But as I peeled back the layers of my discontent, I realized there was something different at the core of my pain. Fear. Fear of completing my journey. My walk was winding down, like a spinning top losing power. My wobble had begun. What was I going to do when my walk was finally over?

It's been said that every new beginning is some other

beginning's end. Perhaps my transition would be more tolerable if I had any real idea of what would come next.

You would think, after all this time on the road with nothing to think about but my next step or the next town, that I would have thought of where I was going. But I hadn't.

I had always thought of my walk as an escape from the past, but now I could see that it was also an escape from my future—a future that I wasn't any more prepared for now than I had been when I first set foot outside my house in Seattle.

Would I ever be ready? Could one really ever be ready for the unknown? If the road has taught me one thing for certain, it is this—one never knows who or what the next mile will bring.

I dried myself off, then went back to my room and lay in bed. The next day likely wouldn't be any better. I disliked walking through big cities, and I was headed straight into downtown Miami.

CHAPTER

Thirty-Two

Thoreau wrote, "The mass of men lead lives of quiet desperation." But on the road, desperation is not always so quiet.

Alan Christoffersen's diary

Not surprisingly, the next morning I was in no hurry to leave the hotel. I easily rationalized that I had pushed myself the day before so I deserved a lighter day. Besides, the room was paid for until noon. I ordered room service, then, after breakfast, went to the pool area and relaxed in the hot tub. I decided to ignore the questions that had troubled me the night before. I still had plenty of miles to torture myself.

It was a little after eleven when I left the hotel. Donning my pack, I walked west on Hallandale Beach Boulevard, west over a coral pink bridge, then headed south again on US 1.

At the first stoplight there was a group of men standing around the intersection collecting money. They wore pink T-shirts that read HOMELESS VOICE. I must have looked homeless, because they didn't ask me for a donation. They didn't offer me any help, either.

After several hours, I stopped for a late lunch at the Dogma Grill—which was basically a fancy hot dog stand. I had a Reuben dog, with melted Swiss cheese and sauerkraut, and an El Macho dog, with spicy salsa, brown mustard, melted cheddar, and diced tomatoes and jalapeños.

When I looked around the place I noticed that as a white man I was a minority, which I'd gotten more used to in the South. Since walking through this part of the country, I'd had some thoughts on America's racial makeup.

In *Travels with Charley* John Steinbeck wrote:

> Americans are much more American than they are Northerners, Southerners, Westerners, or Easterners . . . California Chinese, Boston Irish, Wisconsin German, yes, and Alabama Negroes, have more in common than they have apart . . . The American identity is an exact and provable thing.

I don't know if this is still the case in America. I may be wrong, but it seems that there may be some unraveling of the American tapestry. I see people getting so caught up in celebrating diversity that they are neglecting their commonality. I don't see this as a good thing. The Chinese culture has survived for more than five thousand years in part because the Chinese have embraced the same language and culture.

I hope I am wrong about this, and that the flame is still on beneath the great American melting pot. Americans need each other, and a house divided, no matter the color of its occupants, is still divided. And divided we all fall.

∾

I finished my meal, then headed back out to the street. Like those of most American metropolises, Miami's outskirts were scattered with the homeless, and I walked past people sleeping on benches and underneath overpasses.

Around four p.m. I entered the heart of the city. It was close to rush hour, and the traffic was thick. The roads looked more like parking lots than thoroughfares, and, for once, I had an advantage over the car-bound.

I didn't log as many miles as usual, but I'd gotten a late start, and city walking was always slow. I spent the night at the outskirts of the city at Hotel Urbano—a funky little sixty-five-room hotel in a residential area. I had promised Nicole that I would let her know when I reached Miami, so just before going to bed I called her.

"Hi, handsome," she said. "Where are you?"

"Miami," I said.

"So what day will you cross the finish line?"

"I'm about eight days out."

"Today is the fifth, so you'll reach Key West on the thirteenth. That means we'll have to fly out the afternoon of the eleventh, spend the night in Miami, then drive down the next day. That will put us in Key West the evening before."

"That sounds good," I said. "It will be good to see you."

"I can't wait to see you," she said. "Can you believe you're almost there?"

"No. I can't. It feels surreal."

"It's going to be fantastic," she said. "Should I alert the Key West newspaper?"

"Absolutely not," I said.

"All right. Just your two favorite girls."

"Travel safe," I said.

"You do the same," she replied. "I love you."

"I love you too."

We hung up. If it wasn't for Nicole, there would be no one. What if I had walked all that way and no one noticed? I suppose it would be like writing a book, then burning it before anyone read it.

CHAPTER

Thirty-Three

If God came to save the world, why are so many of His professed followers intent on damning it?

Alan Christoffersen's diary

The hotel offered breakfast in the lobby, and I poured myself a cup of coffee, then prepared two packages of instant oatmeal that I topped with brown sugar and sliced bananas. As I was finishing my breakfast a man, thirtyish with a narrow face and a light beard, approached me. "Have you found God?" he asked.

I looked at him for a moment, then replied, "I didn't know He was lost."

The man stared at me stoically. "I'm from the Miami Church of Christ Risen, the only true church on the earth."

"The *only* true church?" I repeated.

He read my skepticism and replied, "Obviously there can be only one truth. I've heard fools say that churches are like spokes on a wheel, all leading to the same place, but anyone with half a brain knows that can't be right. Truth isn't duplicitous. You don't tell a mathematician that there's more than one answer to a math problem—either you get it right or you don't, and the level of a person's sincerity or commitment doesn't change the truth an iota." He leaned toward me. "Has the truth saved you?"

"That depends on what you mean by *truth*," I said.

"If you are not living the doctrine of truth, you cannot be saved."

"You mean the 'truth' your church teaches."

"Yes, sir."

"And only those in your church are saved?"

"That is correct."

"Then I guess not. How many are in the Miami Church of Christ Risen?"

"We are growing rapidly," he said, his voice becoming animated. "We have nearly five hundred."

"That many," I said, couching my sarcasm. "So the other seven billion plus inhabitants on this earth . . ."

"Lost."

"Lost," I repeated. "What exactly does that mean?"

"To be lost is to exist eternally in a state of spiritual limbo, lost to God, damned in eternal progression."

"So everyone in the world is lost but you and your five hundred souls."

He nodded.

"Doesn't that seem a little . . . wrong?"

"God is never wrong. God's ways are not man's ways. We don't make the rules. God does. And He does as He, in His infinite wisdom, deems righteous."

I looked at him for a moment, then said, "Actually, I think that you, or whoever runs your church, made up the rules to exalt yourself and damn others. If there is a God, I don't think that would please Him."

He shook his head sadly. "You are lost."

"Well, at least we have that settled," I said. He was looking at me with such an expression of self-righteousness that I wanted to punch him. "Tell me, who is this God you worship?"

"Our God has many names. Elohim, Chemosh—the God of Moab, Yahweh, the only True God."

"And your God is just?"

"Of course."

"And you think it's just that billions of people who were raised differently than you or in other places of the world are not saved?"

"They are the sons and daughters of perdition," he replied. "Unless they repent and come unto Christ, through our church, they cannot be saved."

It was hard for me to believe that he could so easily throw all of humanity under the bus in the name of God. "Your little five hundred represent a grain of sand in the vast beach of human existence. If that is all your god is *able* to save, he is not very powerful. And if it's all he's *willing* to save, then he is certainly not very loving. Frankly, I think you worship a pathetic god."

The man looked at me in horror. "That's blasphemous. I fear for your soul."

"Don't bother," I replied. "Your god doesn't scare me. I'll stick with a god who is great enough to love all his creation."

I finished my coffee, picked up my pack, and started out of the hotel, leaving the man and his god behind.

US 1 again became the South Dixie Highway as I reached the town of Coconut Grove. The most unique thing about the town was that the traffic lights were horizontal instead of vertical, something I hadn't seen anywhere else on my walk.

That night, as I ate dinner at a Mexican restaurant, I looked over my map. At my current pace I would reach Key West in just seven days. Walking through the Florida Keys would be unlike any walking I had done elsewhere in the country.

The Florida Keys consist of more than seventeen hundred islands, though only forty-three of them are connected by bridges. I would cross forty-two bridges on my way to Key West, including the longest bridge of my walk, the Seven Mile Bridge.

The keys' history is as colorful as their landscape. Because of their location, the keys have always been a hot spot for drug smuggling and illegal immigration. In response to these problems, in the early 1980s the US Border Patrol created a series of roadblocks to search cars returning to the Florida mainland.

When the measures began to affect Key West's tourism industry, Mayor Dennis Wardlow declared Key West an independent and sovereign nation, renaming it the Conch Republic and appointing himself its prime minister. Wardlow's first act as prime minister was to declare war on the United States, then, in the same hour, surrender and apply for a billion dollars in foreign aid.

Hunter Thompson was right.

CHAPTER

Thirty-Four

I have entered the Florida Keys. If I listen
carefully, I can hear the first musical strains
of the movie credits beginning to roll.

Alan Christoffersen's diary

The next morning I began walking around eight, stopping an hour later at a McDonald's to eat. Shortly after I left the United States mainland. The road changed to two lanes divided by a waist-high, blue concrete median. There was a wide, grassy shoulder on each side hemmed in by a tall chain-link fence.

The scenery remained the same all day: black-gray asphalt, a green shoulder, and miles of blue ocean infested with mangrove forests. At around twenty-four miles I entered Monroe County and left the highway at Pirate Hat Marina. After a long and monotonous day, I had hoped for some kind of service, but there were only darkened residences and rental homes. I pitched my tent in a lush, secluded part of the marina and ate dinner from my pack.

I woke early the next morning eager to leave the place. Less than a mile from the marina the highway's name changed to Florida Keys Scenic Highway. I walked through a group of convicts wearing Day-Glo orange jumpsuits who were picking up litter on the side of the road. The men pretty much acted as if I were invisible, except for the two correctional officers who were managing the detail. They watched me closely.

I realized that I had spent the night in the first of the Florida Keys: Key Largo. To tell the truth, I knew of Key

Largo only from the Beach Boys' mention of it
"Kokomo," which they supposedly wrote on the

Billboards advertising scuba diving and sn
tours flanked both sides of the highway, which
you would expect in the self-proclaimed "diving
of the world."

I stopped at a Circle K for something to eat and
look for a more detailed map of the keys. I asked t
female clerk if there were many hotels in Key West, bu
she didn't know. In fact, she said that she had never been
there. I was surprised, even more so when she told me
that she had lived in the Florida Keys her entire life. I
asked her if she ever planned to visit Key West, and she
just shrugged. "I don't know," she said. I wondered why
someone would choose to live in such a small world.

She gave me a free map and a Key West coupon
book. I bought some sunscreen, an orange, and an egg-
and-cheese breakfast burrito, then sat down to eat as I
looked over the map. From what I could see, many of the
keys seemed nearly deserted, and I would be camping
some nights.

By evening, I had logged twenty miles, ending at the
district of Tavernier. I booked a room at the Historic Tavernier Inn, a tiny hotel on the east side of the thorough-
fare, then ate dinner at the Café Cubano, a homespun
diner run by a Cuban family. I ate clam chowder and pork
chops, which came with a side dish of sweet plantains,
then retired to my hotel for the night.

The next morning it took me only an hour to make it to
the township of Islamorada, which is technically a village

onsisting of Plantation Key, Windley Key, Upper Mate-
umbe Key, Lower Matecumbe Key, and two offshore
islands.

A little way into the village I came to a long building
with a sign out front that read

HISTORY OF DIVING MUSEUM

I went inside to check it out. There was a sign above
the museum entrance that read

Man has left footprints on the moon but still hasn't walked on the ocean floor

I was the only one there. Even though the museum
was small, it was crowded with exhibits and artifacts that
the owner had spent his lifetime collecting. I thought it
was pretty interesting, especially the deep-sea diving outfits that looked like robots from sixties sci-fi novels.

After the museum I stopped at the Islamorada Restaurant & Bakery—home of the famous Bob's Bunz—for
lunch. I ordered a Reuben o' the Sea sandwich, which was
basically a Reuben sandwich with fish instead of pastrami,
a side of sweet potato fries, slaw, and one of their cinnamon buns.

While I was waiting for my food I read about the
bakery's history, which was printed on the back of their
menu. The bakery's owner was a Philadelphia native who,
some twenty years ago, had come to the keys for a season
and never left. It was something I could understand.

More than once I had fantasized about reaching Key
West and never leaving. Of course that's all it was—a
fantasy. I had no idea what I'd do there. A city as small

as Key West could never support an advertising agency or even a single ad guy. Maybe I'd buy a fishing boat and take tourists out. I'd name my boat the *McKale*. Of course I would. When people asked who McKale was, I'd tell them she was a beautiful girl in a dream I once had and leave the rest to their imaginations.

I finished my meal, then started off again. At fourteen miles I reached Indian Key. It was narrow enough that I could have easily thrown a stone from one side of the key to the other. There were cars parked alongside the road, and people had gotten out to swim in the ocean.

The next key was the Lower Matecumbe Key. It was linked to Long Key by a long bridge with dozens of people fishing from it.

The sun was setting as I reached my day's destination, Fiesta Key and the Fiesta Key RV Resort, a twenty-eight-acre RV park. I was tempted to stay in one of their cottages overlooking the sea, but the price the guy in the rental office quoted me was too much—$250 per night with a two-night minimum. For five hundred dollars I would sleep in my tent again.

I rented a small campsite, about fifteen by fifteen feet, marked by oiled railroad ties. Even with sleeping in my tent, the park was more luxurious than most of my camping; there was a pool, bathrooms, a laundry, a mini-mart, and a small diner called the Lobster Crawl Bar & Grill.

I set up my tent while there was still light. Then I put a load of whites in the washing machine and went to dinner at the restaurant. I had calamari rings, coconut shrimp, and a mushroom Swiss burger.

Then I went back to the Laundromat and put my whites in the dryer. No one else was using the place, so I left my clothes and went back to my tent to sleep.

CHAPTER

Thirty-Five

Today I crossed one of the longest bridges in the world—a fitting, though trite, metaphor for the completion of my walk.

Alan Christoffersen's diary

The next day's walk was more of the same—more keys, more ocean, more bridges. An hour and a half into my walk I reached the Long Key Channel Bridge, which was the longest I'd encountered in the keys so far, almost two and a half miles, spanning south to Conch Key. There was a narrow pedestrian lane, but I was the only one using it. The turquoise water below looked inviting, but I remembered once seeing a video of a massive hammerhead shark stealing a fisherman's catch in the Long Key Channel, which was reason enough to stay on the bridge.

Next I passed through Duck Key, then Marathon Key, where I ate lunch at a place called The Wreck. Marathon is one of the larger keys, a full residential community with hotels, banks, and schools. I walked the rest of the day on Marathon and spent the night at the Ranch House Motel.

◇

The next morning I ate breakfast at the Wooden Spoon restaurant, where I had coffee and a chili omelet with a side of grits. Less than an hour later I reached the famous Seven Mile Bridge.

Seven Mile Bridge was, at its creation, one of the

longest bridges in the world, connecting Knight's Key to Little Duck Key. Near its center, the bridge rises in an arc to sixty-five feet, high enough to provide clearance for boat traffic. Like the Long Key bridge, Seven Mile Bridge has a narrow pedestrian lane, its outer edge flanked by concrete safety barriers. It took me about an hour and a half to cross the bridge, and, in spite of the danger inherent in walking such a narrow space, the view was worth the hike.

To the east of the bridge was the remnant of the older bridge (with the unfortunate name of Knights Key–Pigeon Key–Moser Channel–Pacet Channel Bridge), which had been constructed in the early 1900s by Henry Flagler but had been damaged by the Labor Day Hurricane of 1935—the most intense hurricane ever to make landfall in the United States.

⟜

Late afternoon I entered Big Pine Key. The key is a preserve for a tiny endangered species called key deer. The road was enclosed on both sides with chain-link fence and posted with deer crossing and myriad endangered species signs. I saw one of the deer as I walked. It was just a few yards behind the fence eating leaves off a bush. The animal seemed to have no fear of humans and didn't even stop to look at me. I don't know if it was an adult or not, but it was barely two feet high at the shoulders.

Even though I had walked less than twenty miles, I stopped for the day. Key West was thirty miles away, with another four or five miles to reach the southernmost end. It was a distance I had walked before, but not easily, and I didn't want to reach Key West exhausted and in the dark, so I broke up the final leg of my journey into two trips of twenty and ten miles.

I booked a room at the Big Pine Key Motel, and the man at the front desk suggested that I eat dinner a few blocks away at the unoriginally named Big Pine restaurant. I ordered a mixed green salad, fried clams, and the HE-MAN ribs.

As I was finishing my meal I checked my watch. If their flight wasn't delayed, Nicole and Kailamai should have landed in Miami almost two hours earlier. They planned to stay in a hotel near the airport, then rent a car and drive to Key West in the morning, passing me somewhere along the way. The thought of mixing my two worlds seemed a little surreal. I turned on my phone just in case they called.

I was grateful that they were coming and that someone, besides me, would witness the end of my walk. Still, I couldn't believe my walk was finally at its end.

CHAPTER

Thirty-Six

Nicole and Kailamai have arrived in Key West.
I realize that I have compartmentalized my
life, as it's peculiar having them here. It's like
daddy-daughter day at the office.

Alan Christoffersen's diary

I woke with the realization that it was my last full day of walking. I ate breakfast at a café called the Cracked Egg. I had coffee, orange juice, and their specialty, the Gut Buster—potatoes covered with shredded cheddar cheese, sausage gravy, and two scrambled eggs.

My phone rang while I was eating. It was Nicole.

"Good morning, handsome," she said brightly.

"Good morning," I replied. "Are you in Miami?"

"Yes, we're just leaving the car rental. The man at the counter said it would probably take us about three and a half hours to reach Key West."

"It took me a bit longer than that," I said.

"I'm sure it did. Where are you?"

"I'm on Big Pine Key. So, in three and a half hours you'll probably catch me around Sugarloaf Key. You won't miss me—I'm the guy with the big pack walking along the side of the road."

"I can't wait," she said. "I'll try not to hit you."

"Much appreciated," I replied.

⌒

By lunchtime I had passed through a series of small keys with interesting names: Little Torch Key, Big Torch Key, Ramrod Key, Summerland Key, and, finally, Sugarloaf

Key, where I was passed by a young woman wearing a blue polka-dot bikini and driving a mint-green scooter with a cooler on the back. She personified the uninhibited spirit I expected of the islands. She looked like a party waiting to happen.

Around two o'clock I was passing by Sugarloaf Shores when I heard a car horn honking behind me. I turned back to see a bright yellow Mustang convertible with its top down, flashing its lights. It took me a moment to realize it was Nicole and Kailamai. They slowed by my side and blew kisses, then pulled off the road, jumped out of the car, and ran to me.

"You made it," I said.

"We went topless the whole way," Kailamai said.

Nicole shook her head. "The car top was down," she said. "Which is why I look like I did my hair in a wind tunnel."

I shrugged off my pack and hugged the women.

"The weather is so nice here," Nicole said. "I can't believe it's December."

"It's like twenty degrees in Spokane," Kailamai said. "I think I'm moving here after school."

"How far have you walked today?" Nicole asked.

"About fourteen miles," I said.

"Where will you be stopping for the day?"

"In about six more miles. Saddlebunch Keys."

Nicole processed the information. "Okay, we'll go on to Key West and check into our hotel, then I'll book a restaurant in Saddle . . . back . . ."

"Saddle*bunch*," I said.

"Saddlebunch," she repeated. "That's an odd name. Anyway, I'll make reservations and we'll have dinner together. How long will it take you to get there?"

"Maybe an hour and a half," I said.

"Okay, we'll hurry." She hugged me again. "It's so good to see you. We're so excited for you."

"Yeah, you're the man," Kailamai said. "The walking man."

I waved at them, watched their car disappear, then picked up my pack and trudged on after them.

❧

Nicole called me an hour later. "We're checked in," she said. "We're staying at the beachside Marriott. It's not even fifty yards from the entrance to Key West. The clerk helped me make reservations at a restaurant called Kaya Island Eats. I said we'd be there at six fifteen."

"About forty-five minutes," I said, looking at my watch. "That's good. I'm about a half hour from Saddle-bunch Keys right now. Where's the restaurant?"

"It's on the highway, so you'll pass right by it. But we'll wait out front for you. Kailamai and I are headed there right now."

"I'll see you there," I said.

I put my phone back in my pocket. It took me about forty minutes to reach the restaurant. As I approached I could see Nicole standing alone out front, next to the Mustang.

"Where's Kailamai?" I asked.

"She's inside. They seated us a little early."

"Can I put my pack in the car?"

"Of course." I stored my pack in the trunk, and we went inside. Our table was next to a large window and had a beautiful view of the Gulf of Mexico. Kailamai was holding a drink with a pink umbrella.

"What are you drinking?" Nicole asked.

"Piña colada," Kailamai said. "Don't worry. It's virgin."

"It better be."

Kailamai smiled at me. "How was your walk?"

"You mean from Seattle or from Sugarloaf Key?"

"Both."

"Long," I said. I pulled out Nicole's chair, and she sat down. Then I sat between the ladies.

"I bet you're hungry," Nicole said.

"Famished." I looked over the menu. The selections were as colorful as the restaurant. I ordered the Chicken Cherryaki, chicken covered with teriyaki sauce and black cherry preserves, and Scott's Tomato Salad with Mozzarella and Mascarpone. Kailamai ordered the Jamaican Jerk Wings with goat cheese, and Nicole had the No Worries Shrimp Curry, glazed shrimp with coconut red curry sauce.

Nicole also ordered a bottle of wine. The wine list was the most interesting I'd ever seen, and she ended up selecting a bottle called Hey Mambo Kinky Pink Rosé, which claimed to taste like strawberries, soft plums, and apricots.

She poured the wine, then lifted her glass to me. "We should toast the completion of your walk."

"It's too soon," I said.

"It ain't over until the fat lady crosses the finish line," Kailamai said.

Nicole grinned. "I think you said that wrong."

"I saw this YouTube video of a bike race. About fifty feet before the finish line the guy who's in first place raises his hands to celebrate his victory, but his tire hits something and he crashes. By the time he gets going again, the second- and third-place guys have crossed the finish line."

"I get it," Nicole said. "No premature celebrating. Then what should we toast?"

"How about the two of you being here with me?" I said.

"That works," she said. "To being together."

"And the sun," Kailamai added. "It's pretty nice too."

"And the sun," I said.

We clinked each other's glasses. The wine was as fruity as promised. Nicole's phone rang, and she checked to see who was calling. "I need to take this," she said. "I'll be right back."

I looked at Kailamai. "Sounds important."

Kailamai just shrugged, then asked, "What time will you reach Key West tomorrow?"

"I'm not sure. Probably around noon. When our waitress returns I'll ask exactly how many miles we are from Key West."

It was about five minutes before Nicole returned. "Sorry about that," she said, sliding into her seat.

"Is everything okay?" I asked.

"Everything's fine," she said, smiling.

Our waitress came over to the table with our food. She set down our plates, then asked, "Does everything look all right?"

"Everything looks beautiful," Nicole said.

"Great. Anything else?"

"I have a question," I said. "About how far are we from Key West?"

"Not far," she said. "It's just down the road. About twenty minutes."

"He means walking," Kailamai said.

She looked back at me. "No, it's too far to walk. I could call you a taxi."

Nicole said, "He just walked all the way here from Seattle."

She looked back at me. "Across the country?"

I nodded.

"In that case, it's really close. Maybe eleven miles."

"Thank you," I said.

She walked away.

"How long will that take you?" Nicole asked.

"A little less than three hours. I'll probably start a little later."

"So, depending on when you leave, you'll reach Key West by early afternoon."

I nodded. "That's about right."

"I still can't believe you're really here," Kailamai said. "Do you remember our first day walking together? I had never even heard of Key West. I asked you if you knew how to get there."

I smiled. "Yes. That was right before you asked me if I believed in aliens."

"You remember that?"

"How could I forget? You had a theory that aliens are really just humans in the future, so they aren't traveling in spaceships but time machines."

"I can't believe your memory," Kailamai said. "You've got to admit it makes sense."

"I remember the first time I saw you," Nicole said. "I was just outside Waterville with a flat tire."

"You had lost your lug nuts," I said.

She grinned. "That sounds rude."

I laughed. "Then you told me that you didn't need any help because your husband was on his way."

"What was I supposed to say? I was completely alone when this long-haired, unshaven stranger shows up out of nowhere . . . even though you were pretty gorgeous."

"I'm glad you got that flat," I said.

Nicole's countenance turned more serious. "Thank God for flat tires."

"Sometimes life is like that," Kailamai said. "Things that seem bad at the time are really blessings."

Nicole took another sip of wine. "Sometimes."

The food was delicious, and after our main course we shared a piece of key lime pie, the first I'd had since reaching the keys. I wasn't used to taking so much time to eat, and it was dark outside when we finished. I asked the restaurant's hostess where I could find the nearest hotel. She replied, "Key West."

"Why don't we just drive to Key West and you can stay at the Marriott with us?" Nicole said. "Then I could just bring you back in the morning."

"You can't do that," Kailamai said. "That would be anticlimactic."

"She's right," I said. "It's okay. I passed a camping area about a mile back. I can do one last night in my tent."

"Can we at least drive you there?" Nicole asked.

"Of course."

I got in the car with them, and we drove back along the highway to where I had seen the camping area. It was on the beach, and the only amenities were a crude, single-pipe shower and concrete fire pits. We set up my tent using the car's lights to illuminate the grounds.

"Remember the night we met?" Kailamai said. "It's hard to believe that we slept together in this very tent."

"You were trusting," I said.

"Why wouldn't I be?" she said. "You'd just saved me from being raped."

"Do you still pray?" I asked.

"Every night. Except now I spend more time thanking God for what I have than asking for what I don't."

"You've always been that way," I said. "That's what I like most about you."

"I thought it was my jokes," she replied.

⸎

After we had finished setting up the tent, we gathered some wood, then lit a fire and sat around it, the orange, lapping flames illuminating our faces. The sky was a brilliant blue velvet with sequin stars.

"This is living," Kailamai said. "You're lucky that you've gotten to do so much of this."

"It's better with friends," I replied.

We sat around the fire and talked for nearly an hour. Finally Nicole said, "It's late; we better let you get some sleep. Kailamai, would you wait in the car for a minute while I talk to Alan?"

She glanced back and forth between us, then stood, "Sure. Good night, Alan."

"Good night," I said.

"See you in Key West." She walked back to the car and got inside.

I turned to Nicole. "You wanted to talk?"

She looked at me with a concerned expression. "Are you okay?"

"Of course. Why wouldn't I be?"

"I've just been worried about you. I don't know what you thought would happen when you finally reached Key West . . . After all this way, I just don't want you to . . ."

"Get my hopes too high?" I said.

"Maybe," she said. "You don't need to know all the answers right now. You know that, right?"

I thought about her question, then said, "Yes, I think so."

"I wouldn't be alive right now if you hadn't decided to walk," she said. "In the end, if all that comes from your walk is saving Kailamai and me, I hope that won't be too disappointing. For us, it means everything." She took my hand. "I'm sure that McKale is very proud of you. And so am I." She leaned forward and kissed me on the cheek. "Whatever happens tomorrow, remember that. And don't lose hope. Things have a way of working out." She smiled. "Good night, Alan."

"Good night."

"Call when you're an hour out. We'll be waiting for you at the WELCOME TO KEY WEST sign."

She turned and walked to the car. I watched the taillights disappear. Then I sat down next to the dying fire thinking about what she had just said and wondering if I really believed it.

CHAPTER

Thirty-Seven

Last night I had a dream that I reached Key West. I walked all the way to the southernmost point of the island. When I stepped into the water it was as hard as concrete. So I just kept on walking.

Alan Christoffersen's diary

I woke late the next morning with the sun turning the inside of my tent a brilliant gold. *This is it,* I thought. *Let's finish this.* I rooted through my pack for breakfast but managed to find only a crushed box of frosted strawberry Pop-Tarts, which I ate with a bottle of water.

Call it nerves, but I still wasn't ready to go. There was no one else at the campsite, so I took off my clothes and waded out into the ocean. I sank to my chest in the crystal blue waters, riding the smooth rocking of the waves. My body had changed. I was lean and strong, a far cry from the shape I'd been in during my advertising days.

I had seen America as few ever would. I had walked thirty-five hundred miles through forests, swamps, and mountains, small towns with silly names and big towns with lonely people, apple, orange, and pecan orchards, corn and cotton fields. They say that before you die your life flashes before you, and in some ways that's what I felt like then.

It was nearly noon when I rinsed myself off, dressed, and packed my tent. I strapped on my pack and started off for the last time.

～·

The next twelve miles passed quickly. The traffic grew heavier. There wasn't much to see along the way, or perhaps the scenery was just obscured by the density of my thoughts. It was nearly three o'clock when I spotted the sign.

At the entrance to Key West there is a grass island about the size of a small parade float separating the incoming and outgoing traffic. In the middle of the island is a large, colorful sign that reads:

WELCOME *to*

KEY WEST

PARADISE USA
The Rotary Club of Key West

About the same time I saw the sign I heard Kailamai screaming and saw her waving frantically. A few cars, caught up or confused by her excitement, honked their horns. Kailamai and Nicole were standing on the right shoulder of the road beneath a line of trees.

When I reached the sign I was filled with emotion. The women ran up to me. I shrugged off my pack and embraced them. Nicole began crying. "You did it! You made it to Key West!"

I took a deep breath and let the moment sink in.

"Let's party!" Kailamai said.

"I'm not done yet," I said.

She looked at me quizzically. "What?"

"My goal was to walk as far from Seattle as I could. I'm not there yet. I need to walk to the southernmost tip."

"That bites," Kailamai said.

"May we walk with you?" Nicole asked.

"I'd like that," I said. "But I need to get some lunch. Have you eaten?"

"Just an hour ago," Nicole said. "But that's okay, we'll watch you eat."

❧

We were standing right next to a restaurant, the Tavern N' Town, but they weren't open for lunch, so I put my pack in the trunk of Nicole's car and we walked around the back of the Marriott hotel to the poolside bar—the Blue Bar. I ordered drinks and a fruit plate for the women and a bowl of conch chowder and a prime rib panini with coleslaw for me.

"How was your hotel?" I asked Kailamai.

"Good," she said. "How was your tent?"

"You know, room service was lacking. But I think I might miss it."

Suddenly she started laughing.

"What's so funny?" I asked.

"Check out that sign."

Mounted next to me on the wall was a picture of a chicken standing in the middle of a highway. Written in the sky above the chicken were the words

I dream of a day when a chicken can cross the road without having its motives questioned.

Nicole and I laughed as well.

"I have one," Kailamai said. "Why did Alan cross the country?"

I looked at her and smiled. "To get to the other side."

The real answer would take me years to completely understand.

❧

While we ate, Kailamai did most of the talking, filling us in on her classes, her teachers, and every detail she could remember about Matt, the boy she was dating—he was a Libra, spoke German, and came from Butte, Montana, which she decided must be some kind of a sign, as that was where I had first connected Kailamai and Nicole.

Kailamai rambled on like a radio talk-show host, and the truth is I heard only half of what she was saying. My mind was elsewhere. I could tell that Nicole understood where I was at. She just silently watched me, occasionally interjecting with Kailamai when I didn't respond to something.

After an hour I paid the bill, then stood. "Let's go," I said. We walked to the front of the hotel. "I need to get my pack."

"Why don't you just leave it in the car?" Nicole asked.

"It came with me this far, I think it should finish the ride."

We walked back to the parking lot. Nicole popped the Mustang's trunk, and I lifted out my pack.

"How far is it?" Kailamai asked.

"Maybe four miles," I said.

"Four miles," she said. "That far?"

"I've sleepwalked farther than that," I said.

"Now you're just showing off," she replied.

We walked west across the Marriott's parking lot, then out along the northern split of Highway 1. To our right was the gulf and the lapping water on the shore. In many places the water was thick with mangrove trees.

There are a lot of cyclists in Key West. Most of the bikes looked like antiques, recycled, rebuilt, and resurrected over and over again. I'm sure Hemingway's bicycle is still in rotation out there somewhere.

The cyclists weren't especially attentive to us in spite of the many signs warning cyclists to yield to pedestrians.

We walked past seven hotels the first mile, two of which were closed for renovations.

"Check these out," Kailamai said. She lifted a pair of men's shorts off the sidewalk. "Someone lost their shorts."

"Don't touch them," Nicole said.

"It's Key West," I said, which seemed explanation enough.

In the second mile we passed two white herons standing on the bank. They were beautiful birds, and for a moment we all just looked at them. Then Nicole said, "The white heron symbolizes peace." She turned to me. "It's a good sign."

The herons weren't the only birds we saw. There were wild roosters and chickens everywhere.

"What's with all the chickens?" Nicole asked.

"They're protected," Kailamai said. "There's a five-hundred-dollar fine for harassing them."

"How do you know that?" I asked.

"I read it," she said.

"Where did they come from?" Nicole asked.

"Cuba," Kailamai said. "They're Cuban chickens."

"I'm sure they're all US citizens by now," I said.

॰ঌ৹

Near the Parrot Key Hotel & Resort, road construction forced us to cross to the other side of the street. We walked past a Pizza Hut building that had been turned into a medical clinic, then we turned off onto Roosevelt, then Truman, which led us into a residential area.

A rusted Toyota pickup truck drove past us, then

stopped about twenty yards ahead of us where a red and gold sofa was sitting near the curb. A thin, balding man got out and opened his tailgate, then walked over to the sofa. Then he just stood there for a moment looking at it. As we approached I could see a handwritten sign that read

FREE. TAKE ME.

Mustering his strength, the man lifted one end of the sofa and began dragging it to his truck.

"Would you like some help?" I asked.

He looked at me with relief. "Yes, thank you."

Kailamai lifted the front of the sofa with the man while Nicole and I lifted the other end. They set their end on the tailgate, then the man hopped up into the truck's bed and began pulling while Nicole and I pushed our end forward. The sofa was longer than the truck's bed and hung out a few feet.

"It's too long," Kailamai said.

"It's all good," the man replied. "Thank you."

"Don't mention it," I said.

We continued walking. We turned south at White Street and walked past the National Weather Service building. I stopped to read the plaque they had posted out front, a memorial to the sixty people who drowned in the 1846 "Havana" Hurricane.

I walked another half block, then saw it. There was ocean, straight ahead of me.

CHAPTER

Thirty-Eight

There are few precious moments in life that we can look up to the universe and say "It is done." This is one such moment. My walk is over.

Alan Christoffersen's diary

We continued on toward the water, and a block later we crossed the street to a long, sidewalk-skirted sandy beach. We had reached Higgs Beach along the south bank, but we still weren't at the southernmost end of the island, which, I knew from the myriad of pictures I'd seen of Key West, was prominently marked with a buoy.

We continued to walk west along the oceanfront until the road turned north on Reynolds, which we followed to South Street, then turned west again. We walked five blocks along South until we reached the southern end of Duval. Again, I could see the ocean ahead of us and a small gathering of people, crowded around the famous southernmost buoy.

On the southwest corner of Duval and South was the Southernmost House inn. There was a gift shop at the west end, and a sign out front had a picture of a pirate next to the words

I went on a rum diet. So far I've lost three days.

Just a few yards ahead of us was the iconic ten-foot concrete buoy, painted red, white, black, and yellow. At the top of the buoy was a large yellow triangle with a drawing of a conch shell in its center surrounded by the words

THE CONCH REPUBLIC

Beneath it were the words

90 MILES TO CUBA
SOUTHERNMOST POINT
CONTINENTAL
USA
KEY WEST, FL

In spite of its fame as Key West's most popular tourist site, the buoy is basically a farce. First, it's not, as it claims, really the southernmost point of the continental United States. Another island, Ballast Key, is even farther south. The buoy is not even the farthest point south in Key West, as some of the shore around it is obviously farther. Second, it's not really ninety miles to Cuba, since Cuba is ninety-*four* miles away. And third, the structure isn't really even a buoy. It's actually an old concrete sewer junction that was too heavy to move, and since the original southernmost sign kept getting stolen, the city painted the junction to look like a buoy.

Notwithstanding the fraud, there was a gathering of tourists taking turns having their pictures taken next to the buoy.

"We've got to take your picture with it," Nicole said.

"All right," I said. The three of us took our place in line. When it was our turn, I walked up to the buoy and, still wearing my hat and pack, leaned back against its cool, rough surface, raising my fingers in a victory sign. "How's this?"

Nicole held up her phone and took a picture. "Perfect," she said.

"Take one with me," Kailamai said.

Nicole took several pictures of the two of us, then said, "Let's get one with all three of us." She turned to the man standing in line behind her. "Would you mind taking our picture?"

"No worries," he said with an Australian accent.

She handed him her phone. "Just push this button."

"Brilliant," he said.

The women stood at my sides while the man snapped picture after picture with Nicole's phone. Finally, after six or so shots, Nicole said, "Thank you. I think that's enough."

❧

As we walked from the buoy Nicole looked down at her phone, then texted something.

Kailamai said, "Well, Al my pal, you've done it. You've walked all the way to the end of the country. You can't go any farther without drowning."

"Actually," Nicole said, glancing over the railing surrounding the buoy, "I think that beach right there is farther south."

I looked out toward it. "She's right," I said. Farther south or not, I liked the idea of the beach. Ever since I had begun, every time I pictured myself reaching Key West I had seen myself walking into the water. "Let's get in the water."

We retraced our steps along South Street, then walked south down a short side road.

The beaches of Key West were not what I had imagined when I first set off, though, to be honest, I had never really given the details of my destination much thought. I had assumed that I would find long white sandy beaches stretching the length of the island, like in Hawaii. Like most things, the dream was greater than the reality. Key West is little more than a coral rock in the sea. If there's sand on the ground, someone likely put it there.

At the end of the road was a strip of sandy beach, surprisingly vacant, which I suspect had to do with both the season and the late hour.

As I walked onto the sand I felt like I was in a dream. I wished it were a dream. I wished I could wake up and look at my beautiful McKale and say, "You'll never believe what I just dreamed."

I slid my backpack off, then sat down in the sand and untied my shoes, which were trashed. They were the seventh or eighth pair since I'd left Seattle—I had lost count. I think my socks were original. At least they looked like they had borne the brunt of thirty-five hundred miles. I peeled them off and threw them aside. Then I stood and turned back. Nicole and Kailamai were standing at the edge of the sand as if they didn't dare step on it.

"Are you coming?"

Nicole shook her head. "This is your moment. We'll wait here."

I took off my hat and threw it on the ground. Then I reached into my pack and pulled out the yellow envelope my father had given me.

I walked to the edge of the water. I stepped onto the firm, wet sand, and the gulf waters rushed over my feet and ankles, cooling them, blessing them for their journey. That's the moment I knew I had reached the end of my walk. That's when I felt my journey end. The realization washed over me as clearly as the water over my feet.

❧

I tore off the end of the envelope, then tilted it, holding my hand beneath the opening. A pinkish-red seashell slid out into my palm. It took me only a moment to recognize what I was looking at. It was the seashell my father had affixed to the plaque in his room—the one I had noticed missing that first night back—the same seashell he'd asked my mother to marry him with.

There were two letters inside the envelope. The first was handwritten on lavender parchment. It was a letter from my mother to my father, written just a week before she died.

February 7, 1988

My dearest heart,

Soon I will sleep. What shall I dream of, my love? I will dream of you, of course. I will dream of you standing in the waters of Key West, your pants rolled up to your knees, and you pointing your little Instamatic at me while I posed for you. I will dream of you lifting that shell and giving it to me and asking me to be yours forever. And, forever, I will kiss you and say "yes."

I will dream of our little boy and his bright eyes and happy smile.

And I will dream for the three of us, a place for us to be, a sanctuary where hearts will never break again. This is my dream, my heart. Never forget that there is no end to us, as there can be no end to love. Love must last forever, or why else would there be love? Until then, I will dream,

Always,

your Kate

Walking on Water

I opened the second letter, which was typed on plain white stationery. This letter was addressed to me.

My Dear Son,

If you are reading this letter it means that I was not able to be with you when you reached Key West. I am sorry for that. It was a hope of mine to see you reach this great goal. You have reached many of your goals, for which I am justly proud. But then I have always been proud of you.

When I lost the love of my life I thought that God or fate or the great cosmic roulette wheel was cruel to make me walk through life alone. But time has brought clarity. I wasn't alone. How grateful I am for the time I have had with you, to see you grow into a man. I have seen you suffer, even as I suffered, and though you never saw it, in dark hours I too have wept for your pain. Son, learn from my mistakes. Don't hold so tightly to the past that you can't hold anything more. Believe in love. Believe that love can last forever. In this I have come to believe that your mother was right all along.

You have completed one journey. I wish you well on the next. And the next. May God watch over you every step of the way.

Love,

Dad

P.S. Please do me this kindness and return this shell to the waters of Key West. It has served its purpose.

My eyes were wet as I folded the letters back together and returned them to my pocket. Then I examined the shell in my hand. It was a little smaller than my palm, ridged and fanned out perfectly, the outer edge a deep red. I held it for a moment, then, as my father had requested, threw it back into the sea. That was it. Life had come full circle.

As the sun continued to sink I looked out over the glowing horizon. "I made it, Mickey," I said. I lifted the chain from around my neck, the one with McKale's wedding ring, and held the ring in my hand. "I did it."

As I looked at the ring I realized just how much I had changed. I remembered holding that ring my fourth night on the road, huddled in the small shack on the east slope of Stevens Pass, as the hail beat down around me. I had clutched the ring as I cried out to McKale, "Why did you make me promise to live?" Now, as I looked at the ring, I understood why.

"I did what you asked, sweetheart. I lived." A strong breeze brushed by.

Perhaps even more important than understanding why, I now understood how. The same way I had walked—one step at a time. My walk had never been about moving on, or moving past my love. I would never be past her. It was about moving forward—even if it were just one step at a time. If I could walk across an entire country, I could do that. My father was right. I had completed only the first of many journeys. Perhaps an even greater journey now awaited me.

"Mickey, if you're here, I want you to know that I love you more than anyone in this world and always will. I will hope that we can be together again. But I won't die in the meantime. There is still life to be lived."

A wave splashed up my shins. I looked down as the water peaked, then receded from the shore. I took a deep breath, then walked back to my pack and sat down in the sand. I took a handful of sand and put it in my pocket for

Walking on Water

Ally the waitress at the 59er Diner. Then I reached into my pack and took out my journal and began to write.

> I made it to Key West. I have walked as far as I could. I have reached the end of my journey only to realize that it is just the beginning.

As I looked over the paper a soft voice behind me said, "I knew you would make it."

I turned around. Falene was standing behind me. A breeze blew her long dark hair, and she pulled a strand back from her face. For a moment we just stared at each other.

"I never doubted you would make it," she said.

I looked at her in disbelief. "Falene . . ." Her gaze was locked on me as I set down my journal and stood. "What are you doing here?"

"Where else should I be?"

I looked at her for a moment, and then I glanced back over at Nicole, suddenly understanding the phone calls she'd been taking. She looked at me and smiled. I turned back to Falene, and for a moment neither of us spoke. Then I asked, "Are you married?"

She slowly shook her head. "No."

"You said you were getting married."

"I also told you that love wasn't everything." She took a step forward, looking more deeply into my eyes. "After you dropped me off at the hotel I cried all night. As soon as I got back to New York I called off the wedding." She nervously looked at me. "I've loved you for so long, I never thought life would give me a chance to be with you. And when it did, I got scared. I didn't feel worthy of happiness." Her eyes welled up with tears. "Am I too late?"

I just looked at her for a moment, then said, "No. You're just in time." Then, for the first time ever, we kissed. And we kissed. After we parted I took her hand. "Come on," I said.

A broad smile crossed her face. "Where are we going?"

I smiled. "Let's go for a walk."

EPILOGUE

Dear fellow sojourner,

It's been more than a year since I last wrote. It's March 4 (no need to read anything into that) and I'm here in the living room of my father's home in California. The weather is beautiful. It's almost always beautiful in Southern California. I suppose that's why so many people live here.

A lot has happened since Key West. Nicole is happy. Her doctor is smitten. He proposed to her a few weeks ago on Valentine's Day, but she's in no hurry to get married, which, of course, only makes him more eager. I think they're a good match. It makes me happy to see Nicole with the love she deserves. There's a side benefit to the doctor (besides free house calls). If they marry, they'll likely move to Pasadena.

Kailamai is doing well. She still hopes to get into law school and to someday be a judge. Or a stand-up comedian. Either way the world will be a better place.

In January I opened an advertising agency here in Pasadena—a new agency with an old name: MADGIC. My first client was the car dealership my father did accounting for. My second was Wathen Development, the company I was pitching the day I learned of McKale's accident.

Things are going well, and I already have as much

work as I can handle. I doubt I'll ever move back to Seattle, even though I have a few clients from there.

Falene is here with me in Pasadena. After she broke off the wedding, the agency dropped her contract. It's one of the best things that has ever happened to her. She's been working with me at the agency and volunteers weekends at a drug rehabilitation clinic for teenagers. I think she's finally starting to believe that she's more than just the girl behind the bleachers.

On New Year's Day, Falene and I went to the arboretum and sat on the same bench we had the night of my father's viewing. I asked her to marry me. She smiled and said, "Why do you think I've been following you around all this time?"

We plan to get married May 3. Someplace indoors. Falene asked if we could honeymoon in Key West. I told her I've been there.

◦◦◦

I think about McKale every day. I suppose that the hole never really goes away, but I've learned that you can fill it with things. Good things. My memories of her are no longer just a source of pain. They are also a fountain of gratitude for the time and love we shared. I still have my days, but I don't think it would be right if I didn't.

◦◦◦

I sometimes think about those angels I met along my walk: Leszek, the Holocaust survivor in Mitchell, South Dakota, who lifted me from the road and taught me how to forgive; Paige, the young woman who rescued me from a tornado outside Jackson City, Missouri; and Analise, the lovely, lonely woman I stayed with in Sidney, Iowa. As I promised, I sent an envelope filled with sand from Key West to Ally, the wise waitress from the 59er Diner near Leavenworth, Washington, and I've spoken twice with McKale's mother, Pamela, who followed me all the way from Custer, South Dakota, to Wall Drug. I am grateful for each of them and the role they played in my journey.

Every now and then people ask me about my walk. They seem surprised or amazed by it, not seeing that it's really no different than what they do every day. Whether they realize it or not, we are all on a walk. And, like me on my journey, none of us know what experiences we'll face or who we'll meet along our road. The best we can do is set our hearts on a mark in the distance and try to make it. For some the road will seem long, while, for others, it will end all too soon. There will be days of clear skies and pleasant walking, and there will be long, bitter stretches trudged through storms. But either way we must walk. It's what we were made for.

I have fulfilled my final promise to McKale. I am living. But the journey seems different to me now. I suppose that the trail never changes as much as the traveler.

When we are young, the road seems so sure and firm. We tell ourselves that we have tomorrow—then we waste our todays in fear of what might be and regret of what wasn't. And we miss the truth that the road is an illusion, and that there are no guarantees of a new day—there never have been, there never will be.

In the end, it is not by knowledge that we make our journeys but by hope and faith: hope that our walk will be worthy of our steps and faith that we are going somewhere. And only when we come to the end of our journeys do we truly understand that every step of the way we were walking on water.

A Letter from the Author

I'm sometimes asked how I came up with the idea for The Walk series. The simple answer is, I was walking. The better answer is that I was walking the four-mile dirt road to my ranch near Zion National Park when the idea came to me to write a story about a man walking across America. The mental conversation that followed went something like this:

Why did the man cross America?
I don't know.

Does he really need a reason?
I've always wanted to walk across America.

Then why don't you?
Because I'm married, I have a family, a home, a job. I'm tied down to responsibilities.

What if you lost all that?

That's when the potential of the series hit me: if you take away everything a man lives for, then what does he live for? That was a question worth writing about.

～

As I sat down to write this story, I soon realized it could not happen from my den; I would have to make the journey myself. I asked my eldest daughter and writing assistant, Jenna, if she would make the trip with me, and she happily agreed. I hadn't realized at the time what a blessing it would be to drive from coast to coast with my daughter.

Driving more than three thousand miles across America was a remarkable adventure. In Yellowstone we were trapped in a herd of buffalo. In Missouri we were forced to take shelter from a tornado. We stopped in the hometowns of people who have changed the world. We walked through fields of potatoes, corn, and cotton, hiked through canyons and swamps, and even held alligators. We climbed lighthouses and walked through cemeteries at night. We took notes in hospitals and met scores of people who shared with us their life stories. One of our most interesting interviews was with Israel, a hitchhiker we picked up outside Hannibal, Missouri, who shared his experience of fourteen years on the road and taught us the difference between tramps, hobos, and mountain men.

～

But all journeys must come to an end. After five years of writing and researching The Walk, the emotions that crossed my heart when I reached the Key West sign were a powerful mix of accomplishment, finality, and nostalgia. I was grateful that I had made the choices that led me to the end of this road—literally as well as figuratively.

It's difficult for me to completely fathom how much this series has meant to many of my readers. Ultimately, The Walk is about hope, and on multiple occasions I've heard how the series has interrupted someone's plan to commit suicide. I've seen tough old men, war veterans, cry as they told me how the series had given them hope to carry on after losing their sweethearts.

And we've had dozens of people call from their deathbeds wanting to know how the series ends before they die.

To all those reading this series, whatever city or country you're in, thank you for joining me on this sojourn and search for meaning and hope in a vast, mysterious world. I hope you have enjoyed the read. But even more, I hope it has brought some illumination to help you on your journey along the difficult and unsure paths of life that each of us must walk.

Sincerely,

Richard Paul Evans

*R*ichard **Paul** Evans is the #1 bestselling author of *The Christmas Box* and *Michael Vey*. Each of his more than twenty novels has been a *New York Times* bestseller. There are more than seventeen million copies of his books in print worldwide, translated into more than twenty-four languages. He is the recipient of numerous awards, including the American Mothers Book Award, the *Romantic Times* Best Women's Novel of the Year Award, the German Audience Gold Award for Romance, three Religion Communicators Council Wilbur Awards, the *Washington Times* Humanitarian of the Century Award, and the Volunteers of America National Empathy Award. He lives in Salt Lake City, Utah, with his wife, Keri, and their five children.

You can learn more about Richard on Facebook at www.facebook.com/RPEfans, or visit his website, at www.richardpaulevans.com.

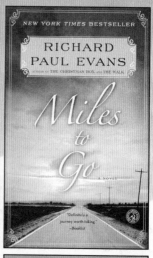
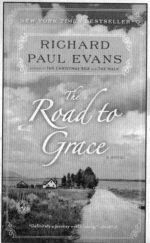
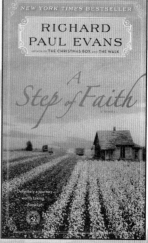